JUST REMEMBER VIOLENCE

ROSS DAVIES

COPYRIGHT

Copy edits by Tristan Robson

Cover photography by Siobhan Alberts (Appearing in the photo from left to right: Sean Martin, Myself, and Tristan Robson)

Cover design by Cassandra Duchesneau

JRV tattoo by Rob Chambers at the Ink Spot at 429 Bank Street Ottawa, Ontario

ISBN-13

978-0986755750

REVISED FIRST EDITION

ACKNOWLEDGMENTS

For starters I'd like to thank Jellybean for convincing me to keep writing. Had you not, I'm not quite sure what I'd be doing right now.

Even though we don't talk, know you were and somehow still are a constant inspiration and I owe you more than I'll ever be able to say. I'd like to thank my parents and family (including Mylan Ly of course) for the unending love and support.

One day, I'll give it back properly.

I'd like to thank Larry Cavanagh and First-Class Press. I'd like to thank my editor Tristan Robson, you're my rock bro, I'm forever in your debt for your friendship and the work you did. Special thanks to Zachary Balloch for being there every step of the way while I wrote Just Remember Violence, thanks bro, you kept me sane.

I'd like to thank Sean(archy) McKay and The Nummies, Brandon James and Kissing With Pop Rocks, Becky Scott, Sean Martin, Eric Lacroix and Sabrina Lesniowski, Pierre Duhaime and Aida Fonseca, Siobhan Alberts and Andrew Lalonde, Chelsea Williams, Crissie Parker, Andrew Goldenberg, Dave Kirkey, Brandy Labine, Veronica Michelle, all my friends and all my acquaintances(sorry I didn't name you), and finally the

Greenspace crew with a special mention to Mike and Andrew.

MY INTRODUCTION

My name is Greyor Allblack, and I remember nothing at all.

That isn't entirely true, that's what they believe. Who are they? They're Grim Associations; my father, mother, and employer. I am the dead man switch.

A memory is something you have, so is a life, so is a dog, lover, even a car. These things can, and maybe, or will, be something you've had. At any time, they can be taken. The question is: can you get them back? This becomes circumstantial; you may have lost them irreversibly, or maybe they were stolen. Something stolen can be taken back, something killed, cannot.

You can ensure a life, a dog, a lover, or even a car.

Does money compensate for their loss?

Grim Associations seem to think so.

And I know what you're asking, what you're thinking, do I agree?

That would have to be a no.

As I said, you can ensure something, something that isn't even a thing, and just because you insure it, doesn't mean you won't lose it, you'll just be compensated when it's gone. If you are one of the unlucky lives that happen to seek or accept insurance through Grim Associations, well, I'm sorry, because you'll never understand the value of those things you insured; you can't, because you're dead, and I'm most likely going to be the one who makes you that way.

Now if you have a dictionary on hand, these are a few examples of insurance:

-The act, system, or business of insuring property, life, one's person, etc., against loss or harm arising in specified contingencies, such as fire, accident, death, disablement, or the like, in consideration of a payment proportionate to the risk involved.

-Coverage by contract in which one party agrees to indemnify or reimburse another for loss that occurs under the terms of the contract.

-The contract itself, set forth in a written or printed agreement or policy.

-Give attention to the sentence where it says, "payment proportionate to the risk involved."

Scary, isn't it?

You know the definition. Know that our company follows it to the last letter, and after that letter, right on and behind the period.

I, Greyor, have little concept of remorse, because remorse extends from compassion, and I am without it.

I, as though a child, don't understand these concepts because I don't remember being a child. I have nothing to base sympathy or remorse on.

I can only see situations, I can't fathom anything else, only what could be, and eventually, what is.

I remember what I'm told to do. I remember my training. I remember violence and nothing else. Or at least I didn't until – well, I'll get to that.

Grim Associations, with the help of a man named Henry Alrick, produced and tested a drug that just so happened to remove one's ability to sustain long term memory without constant levels of the drug in one's system. As a side effect, not only did it remove the ability to sustain long term memory, but it also removed long term memory. Once you're on it, you're who they tell you to be. I was a product of this drug without the nastier side effects like death, full cognitive loss of motor function and brain function. I had no side effects from it, other than the obvious, as if I couldn't remember anything from before it, which, in fact, was its purpose.

However, I sustained my ability to function when the drug was removed. I was the same on it as I was off of it. That made me valuable, and at the same time dangerous, because I wasn't supposed to. I wasn't supposed to create new memories without the drug. For all they knew, I couldn't, which in fact, is a lie. I could, they just didn't know.

All of the other subjects couldn't function at all without the drug; they were vegetables. They'd still, drooling, without any signs of life. I, however, could sit up, pay attention, function entirely, but fake remembering. They'd repeat themselves, testing to see if I could remember what they just told me to do several moments ago, but every time, without fail, I convinced them that I needed the drug to function because if they knew, they'd kill me. It's that simple. Lie to live.

And I did.

Now here begins the question, metaphorically simple: am I lying to live, or am I living a lie?

That's how it began, that question. My purpose would be to answer it, and I did.

CHRISTOPHER HELM

My first policy—my first kill—was a man named Christopher Helm. He'd bought a claim a year and a half ago to cover accidental death or dismemberment. My company insures him. Because of that, tonight, he will die. He is a steel worker—I'd say was, but currently, as I sit staring out the window of my motel, trying to see the street through the rain that obscures the dirty glass—he's still alive.

As I said, I see situation. I don't see, think, or dream of anything else. I'm sitting on a dirty blanket, that's on an even dirtier mattress, contemplating. I guess that'd be the difference between a hotel and a motel; that, or a motel is a one to three story structure with rooms that open to the exterior of the building, usually surrounded by a common balcony or patio, while a hotel has rooms that open to the interior of the building, along a hallway, and is multi-storied.

Or maybe it's because a motel is somewhere you stop for the night to sleep, fuck, or kill somebody. Depends on how you live.

In front of the bed is a crappy television with bunny ears set crookedly on top of it, the television is off, and I'm sitting with my side to it staring out this window, thinking. I'm thinking about Christopher, thinking about killing him, but making it look like an accident.

I know where he lives, where he eats, and where he's going to die.

Christopher has no idea he's going to die, and I still don't know how I'm going to kill him, but I will soon.

I turn my attention to the digital alarm clock on the side table next to the bed and I watch patiently for this hour to pass, focusing on the little red numbers that change shape. When I grow bored of them, I watch the rain again. I watch it pummel and pool on the pavement outside. I can hear people in the next room, so I try to turn my attention from them and listen to the rain, but I can't ignore them as their voices grow louder, louder, and louder until I can't hear the rain.

I hear a girl cry and a man scream. He yells as though she can't hear him; even though she responds, he just yells over her. He accuses her of loving someone else even though she protests that it's him she loves. I hear her wailing as he says he's going to leave and listen as he bangs around their room. She continues to cry, begging him to stay, trying to prove he's being a fool. He doesn't listen, he throws something, and I hear it shatter, then something happens to me.

I try to ignore, refocus, and think about what I'm supposed to think about. Something I don't know distracts me, I feel sick; I know this isn't my business, but I can't help myself. They are now all I can hear; her crying, him screaming and I stand. I turn my head to their wall where the thumping resonates from. I walk over and touch the wall; I can feel their fighting, I can feel their voices, and I feel their pain.

I walk to my door and open it, greeted by the sleet of rain; the smell of fresh air replaces the stale of my room. I walk out on the common balcony and turn toward their room. I walk bare foot and stand in front of their door silently and I listen. The fight hasn't escalated, but it hasn't stopped either. The screaming and crying are constant, the same words being tossed around smothered by one another's disbelief. This fight isn't going anywhere, but it will. It'll either get worse, or end. I'm just impatient.

My handshakes with self-restraint as it goes for the knob. However, my foot doesn't share the same restraint as I kick the door open. My other hand, now armed with my black, suppressed M1911A1. I extinguish the lights in the room with two well placed and extremely quick shots that hiss from the extended barrel.

I move into the room before they comprehend what's going on. I move to where the man was, who I gather is more afraid then angry now. I bring the butt of my gun across his jaw, and he falls hard on to the bed. The girl goes to run but I sweep her feet out and she falls. I pick her up and toss her next to him. I remove my knife and the shine from the blade is the only light in this room now. She whimpers as I pick up a sheet from the floor and cut it down the middle. I climb on the bed and throw her on top of him. She goes to speak but I silence her with a shush and a wave of my knife. I put her on her stomach, on top of him, and tie her hands and feet. I cut more sheets to make her a gag and wrap him up. Finally, I use the last of the sheet to tie them together, facing each other.

I walk back to the door reaching down briefly to pick up the empty casings. I grab the door and close it quietly behind me and go back to my room.

When I get back to the room, the floor right in front of the door is mildly damp from the rain that got in. I curl my toes in the wet carpet and sigh as I listen. Only silence now. I look at the alarm clock, and this hour is almost expired, which means I have to leave now. I remove the pair of rolled up socks from off my bed. I dry my feet on the blanket and grab my boots. I slide my boots on, taking my time lacing each one, pulling the lace tight and then drawing them in a knot when they reach the ankle. The whole time, my eyes never leave the red numbers that click away in the last five minutes of this hour. I smile as I hear nothing. Soon they'll know they're safe, but they'll never fully comprehend why that happened, and I don't understand why I did it. What I do know is, they won't be fighting each other anytime soon, and that's good enough for me.

When that last minute rolls over, and I'm greeted by zeroes, I stand up and make my exit. I turn off the lights and close the door. Walking out into the rain, out on the balcony, walking down the stairs, and over to my car. I'm soaked by the time I reach the door, but I don't mind. I smile as I sit down, thinking about checking out but realized I never checked in as I look up to see the resident of the room, I was stumbling up the wet stairs back to his motel room.

I turn the key and as the car starts, I watch him notice the wet carpet at the foot of his door and he turns around right as I drive away.

I slide my phone open and go over my documentation in the parking lot across from his work site. Christopher Helm, born September 1st, 1978; parents deceased, a wife named Loraine Helen Helm, maiden name Ackers, no children. Christopher has a mistress named Christina Perkins. Sadly, for Loraine, Christina is his primary beneficiary, and Loraine is the contingent.

Poor Loraine.

This work site empties of its occupants as the minutes pass, through my binoculars I see Christopher working away, several stories up with the rain and wind. I have to hand it to him, he's brave.

I exit my car and make my way across the muddy parking lot, sticking to the dark side of the construction site. There is a large fence surrounding the site, warning of the dangers within. Safety instructions plastered every several feet state the need for hard helmets and steel toes. I have steel toes; I just don't have a helmet. This fence separates me from the rising steel structure, so in a sprint, I charge it. Leaping, I catch the top of the fence and kick off the mesh that springs back, throwing myself over.

I land in soft mud, sinking incrementally. I take notice of any movement, any security, or other workers. When it is clear, I run toward the east side of the structure where scaffolds stack on one another, almost as if a second structure was being constructed with wood and pipe. I run toward the closest scaffold and throw myself on it. I stay motionless and examine my surroundings—no one. I begin to climb quickly, from one scaffold level to another, up and up until I reach a main support beam. Christopher is several stories above me welding away, unaware of my presence.

These aren't the safest working conditions, the rain I mean, but if it was that bad, he wouldn't be up there. Then again, that is what they will say at his funeral. Accidents happen.

I quickly launch myself from one beam to another, retaking my balance before moving and climbing to the next level. I make sure while I ascend that I'm out of sight. I'm within earshot of Christopher now and maybe if he wasn't welding, he would hear the footsteps on the steel, but he doesn't. I walk down the support beam directly under him as if I was walking a tight rope. Slowly, I make my way opposite the direction he faces, sparks from his welding rain down around me; these little bright sparks burn bright and then disappear into the sleet of the rain. I throw my hands up on the beam he sits on and pull myself up onto it and when I'm secure, I kneel.

Situation: the easiest way to make this look like an accident is for him to fall, but first his support harness needs to fail. I reach out to where the harness is and very slowly begin to disconnect it. He pauses momentarily and I freeze. Cold and wet, I kneel motionless, holding the strap of his harness as he begins to look around, turning, stopping his weld.

He lifts his mask, turning his head to look back, and as he does this, I disconnect him.

"Christopher?" I whisper.

His head swings back quickly, surprised and shaken. I've startled him.

"What the fuck?"

With a single push, he loses his balance, dropping

his tools. He frantically tries to grab something but instead falls flailing, followed by his tools, plummeting downward off the side without structure, without anything to slow his fall. He watches me stand and the expression that paints his face isn't something you can mime. That is fear, justified fear, without bias or end. What he was afraid of, what we're all afraid of, falling without anything or anyone to catch us. He didn't just fall, he was pushed, and I pushed him. I didn't kill him though, the fall did.

I leap down to a support beam under me, and I freeze as I catch the beam, because I hear the sound of him hitting ground. Barely audible with the rain and wind, but I heard it.

I take a deep breath in and fall to the next beam, I do this again and again, until I'm back to the scaffolds. I stop and look around, sitting atop the hill of scaffolds. I search the construction site, no movement.

I leap off the scaffolds and hit the mud hard and I begin to make my way back to the fence, I look back and smile at my footprints. Trackless tread boots. There are footprints, but they are without identifiable tracks. I look back to the fence, repeat my same motion, sprint, leap, grab the top, and throw myself over.

I look around when I land, no one. I make my way over to the parking lot, walk over to my car, and get inside. I sit there and I can't help but remember Christopher's face and how I was the last person to see him alive. I shake this feeling, this unfriendly, unfamiliar feeling, this awareness. Christopher's last moments were that of surprise and sickness, all the things that must have been running around in his head, in the short moments before he hit the ground. That's all I think about. What was he thinking about? I'm supposed to forget this man, but I won't, because Christopher was the first person I killed for Grim Associations, and he won't be the last. I reach into my pocket, remove my pills, and snap back two; with a dry swallow, they disappear.

I turn the ignition and drive away. But I don't forget.

TRIAL AND ERROR

Remember when I said I had to lie to live? Well, lying to live is not as easy as it sounds, especially when you work for a company that doesn't consider trust a form of reassurance. Your word means nothing unless you can hold on to it while being electrocuted again and again until you lose consciousness, and then again after you've regained it. If you can keep the same story through all of that, well, that is good enough for my company.

I'm wakened by light; bright, artificial light. I'm raised from slumber, pulled from my bed, and dragged out of my excuse for a room. Down a hallway with white-on-white floor tiles that border the aged pale teal walls. Every two feet, I cross under a small, square, buzzing, halogen light. I don't fight the ones that retrieved me from my room because I know this part; this is where I pretend to be thoughtless, still, nothing there, nothing at all. This is what they expect to happen when the meds wear off. When I've returned from each job, they remove the medication from my routine, and I should systematically shut down.

So, I pretend to.

At every bend, a new corridor begins with the same floor, same walls, and same lights. I count each tile, each light, and each corner. I do this systematically every time, something to concentrate on, and something to help fight the anger of being torn from sleep. I want to react every time, for every tile I glance at, every buzzing halogen, and for every corner I'm dragged around, I want to react violently, but I don't. I don't react all the way to the double steel doors with round glass windows in them.

I do react when I'm pulled through those doors because I react when I see the chair. The chair is miserable, warped, dark wood that stems up bolted to the floor. Everyone remembers this, a natural knowing, the fear that settles down when you see it. That little sparkle of fight left in each of our pupils knows something bad or something terrible when they see it, and that's something you do not forget.

I give them a forced grunt of opposition; they know I will. Even when I don't care, because I do remember the chair and what happens in it. I have nothing really to fear. So, I don't, I just look like I do.

They strap me to it by my ankles, by my wrists; they strap my biceps and my calves, and then my head so it sits up firmly, posture perfect. Staring out, ahead of me, straight out, so I can see the whole room. A room with four off-white blank walls, one with a one-sided glass mirror, the kind you can see through when standing on the non-mirrored side. The floor is black, and above there is only one hanging light. In this room, there are medical tables and a heart monitor. As my eyes finally focus from the haze, I realize I'm in sweats, no socks, and no shirt.

I recognize the two that retrieved me; I know them and their names. I just stare on, giving no further recognition of them; I've gone somewhere else in my head. I know that on each medical table there are tools that are never used in this procedure; they are just decoration, or should I say intimidation, to instill fear. I know that soon they will start to attach nodes to me, on my temples, over my chest, the nodes on my temples and on my chest provide different purposes. The ones on my temples will provide a place for the current to be introduced, and the ones on my chest will tell my vitals. At each node's end, a wire will attach me to a different machine. When that machine goes on, I can hear me living, the sound of my pulse mechanically echoed in the room. That is the sound I will focus on because when the other machine goes on, it will send a burst of current into my skull.

That current will attack each nerve individually, or it feels that way, even when it is actually simultaneously assaulting them all. Each part of my body will begin to violently convulse, twist, and contort in ways it shouldn't, but trust me, it will.

I hear the charge take; I ignore its hum, distracting

myself from it. Focus on my pulse, my heartbeat.

"This will be uncomfortable Greyor, but I need you to pay attention. Do you understand?"

"Yes."

One of my retrievers looks at the other while he takes his place to my right with a clipboard and a pen. He then looks back at me and flicks the switch.

The lights dim as pain shreds through me, cutting deep into my nerves, sending my muscles constricting. Violently, my chest and jaw tighten, and I can barely breathe. My eyes try to roll back but the pain forces them open. My lids twitch, my body jerks, my teeth grind, and I feel myself losing consciousness as the pain overwhelms me. Suddenly, in the form of a question, the pain stops.

"What is your name?"

I hear the hum, the current recharges, as the lights brighten, I reply.

"Greyor Allblack."

He quickly writes something down and then looks up from his clip board, I watch his lips form a sentence, and I don't hear it until he's staring at me.

"What do you remember about Christopher Helm?"

The hum is over, so I reply without thinking.

"Nothing at all."

He writes it down and then he looks back to the

other retriever. He slowly nods.

Macro-shock, you know the saying: what you don't know can't hurt you - well, its bullshit, it can, and it will, trust me on this.

Pain, both searing and shattering. It moves through me, pinching the bone, jetting out and into the muscle, through the muscle, and finally through the tissue. But it's not gone, no, it goes back in. Re-entering through what felt like its exit.

I begin to cease gripping the chair, waiting for it to end. I know it won't. I shouldn't, but I do.

The lights have all but darkened and I feel I can't hold on to consciousness, but for some reason, I do.

Another question right before I slip completely, and this question, despite having absolutely no meaning, brings me back.

"How'd he die?"

I know who he's talking about but again, and not for the last, I feign memory.

"How'd who die?"

I spit a question out from between my salivating lips, out from the cracks of my clinched teeth.

He looks up at me, looks back to his clip board, before finally looking at his partner.

I then realize that the hum has ended, and I know with silence and blindly bright light the pain is about to return, but this time I'm defenseless. There is no way to distract myself, this pain will knock me out, and they'll bring me back with it.

Over time, this pain—and I can only hope here—will lose severity.

But it is unlikely.

In that moment, within that thought, the light all but vanishes as I'm riddled by more current. I feel loose and I've lost the will to fight this sear. My skin burns and my saliva boils as I desperately attempt to keep my tongue from between my teeth or from choking on it. Darkness brings relief from the pain as I slip somewhere else, away from these men, and away from this chair.

BRANDON CAIN

Take notice of something for me please, if you're ever out, alone in the night. Listen. You'll hear what I hear right now. When cars have stopped parking, or driving by, listen. The quiet isn't so quiet, in the void of things and people, surrounded by houses, apartments, and maybe even trees.

I'm not asking you to listen to the cars, or the insects, no; I'm asking you to just listen, because if you were—you, unlike Brandon Cain—would hear me coming.

I'm not coming in a sneaking flat black vehicle, headlights off, with my engine quiet, suspiciously rolling down your street with my window half-down ready to drive-by shoot you.

No, I'm on foot. Walking calmly down your street, and if you were listening, you could hear each step get closer, louder and louder, until I'm at your doorstep; but you, like Brandon Cain, wouldn't be listening because you have no reason to. It is easy when you're clueless, clueless that someone is coming to take your life, especially when you've signed it away knowing you need to insure it because somewhere inside of you; you know, you all die sooner than later.

Brandon lives unlike most. Every day to him offers

chance, chance of fortune or chance of loss. Brandon is a gambler. He's bet away his savings, he's gambled away his earnings, all for the chance of winning big. He's made enemies because he owes money. He's lost family because he's borrowed and lost and never paid it back. He's lost the love and the trust of the people around him, and he's got nothing to show for it. But five months ago, when he took the policy, everything changed. He's won money, paid his debts, gained the trust and love of the people around him back, and began working again. Since the day he took that policy, his luck changed. Ironic, isn't it? Knowing Brandon; he won't continue like this, he'll relapse. Good things never last, especially when you make as many bad decisions as he has. Fucking up is almost natural. It is strange because his job requires a certain fragility and patience. He doesn't apply those same qualities to his life and because of that his life and job do not mix well even when he is fantastic at what he does for a living.

Brandon is a glassblower, a professional hot glass artist, and he's good, really good. In fact, I've seen one of his latest pieces. From the kiln, he made a palm-size glass heart. This glass heart was fitted with a silver chain and this heart he gave to his girlfriend, his beneficiary. The heart sparkles and still holds the color it came out of the kiln with, as if the heart was still molten.

This glass heart, so unique, managed to mend the gap between them, and I watched it happen. She had been screaming at him, wanting to know why she should stay, wanting to know why he still was gambling. He stood there and listened to all of it; her frustrations, her worries, her hate for the life that had separated them, and the whole time he stayed silent. No excuse, no words, not even a slight change of expression, all he did was reach into his pocket. All of her anger and noise was silenced when he brought that heart from his pocket, and from his pocket, that silver cord followed. He changed her, right then and there, and all she could do was smile.

I have to admit it saddens me to watch such talent go to waste, because Brandon lives in a house of glass, and I've come to throw stones. Jagged, sharp, and fatal are the stones I bring, and they won't just shatter his home, they'll bring him down with it.

I'm standing on his doorstep, under the cover of his doorway. His porch light's extinguished, standing out in the dark jungle of row houses that illuminate the entrances all looking like the next.

Unlike you and Brandon, I pay attention to the emptiness of the night; I listen attentively and because of this, I hear the clip clop of stiletto heels growing closer. Echoing loudly in the motionless night, and I'm here, without a place to hide, because those noisy heels are making their way here. I turn and look. There, some twenty doorways away, approaching from between cleavage, is the brilliant molten heart hanging seductively on the chest of Brandon's beneficiary. She hasn't seen me, and I intend to keep it that way. I walk off the porch and make way toward the porch next to Brandon's, and I freeze with a word,

"Brandon?"

A soft voice licks out from behind me, beckoning for me to turn and correct her. With that, the heels stop, and she stands there waiting. I turn and smile,

"No, not Brandon."

"Oh, sorry, do you know him? Is he home?" The heels begin again. She grows closer, and I'm paralyzed watching that heart limply bounce from each breast.

"Oh, no, sorry, I don't... Is this his house? Yep, that would mean I'm at the wrong place, again."

I begin to move again and then another question stops me.

"What address are you looking for?"

"Twenty-two thirty-eight."

She giggles and smiles.

"Yeah, you're lost. That's on the other side of the block. You're way off. I can show you if you want."

Without a thought, a smile creeps across my face, even though this isn't funny, and I know where I am, I can't help it. I laugh and for this moment it is sincere, even when it shouldn't be. I shouldn't have even allowed her to see my face, but I can't help it. That grin of mine grows wider and I chuckle.

"No, I'm good, thank you though. I appreciate the offer, but I'll find my way. Have yourself a good night." I smile.

She smiles, tilting her head and she squints.

"Ok then, you too. I'm Becky by the way."

I stand there smiling, staring, without flinching. She stands with her hands on her hips, with her lip between her teeth and as she raises an eyebrow, cocking her head slightly to the right, her fiery hair hangs off her face before she tosses it back waiting for a reply.

Dumbfounded by her presence, I stutter the first sentence that crosses my mind.

"I'm Johnny...It's nice to meet you, Becky."

I smile, pondering my choice of names and how it didn't require a single second for me to make one up; that one came without thought, which causes me to wonder why I chose it. Wayward, I begin to walk away as I hear her heels click in motion toward Brandon's door.

"It was nice meeting you too, Johnny."

She calls from behind me, and again, without thought, I respond.

"You too, Becky. You too."

When I'm out of sight, I stop. I stop moving and stop thinking. I wait as the night passes on, and the hours click away. I have to wait until Becky is gone; she isn't part of this, and I have no claim on her. So, Brandon gets one more night and sure, it'll be worth it. If he knew he was going to die, he'd make it worth it. Wouldn't you?

Or would you do everything in your power to have another night, followed by another, and I'd have to bet you'd pick the latter. I'm sure you're not alone in that regard because if I had a choice in having one last mind-altering, passion-stained night or fighting for my life every day, I'd fight so I could, if I chose to, have night after night of mind-altering, time stopping, completely and totally soaked passion. I don't get the choice of either one, but for some reason, I'd rather just fight. I guess that's why I do this, and then I'm reminded, maybe that's why I'm alone.

PROBLEMS AT THE OFFICE

Say, you're good at what you do. Praise or not you know you're good at it. Say, if you stop, maybe suddenly or maybe not so suddenly—stop—being good at what you do. Focus on that feeling for a second, when and if that happens to you, if it hasn't already happened. It's not a good feeling. If you stopped being good at your job, whatever your job is, you get fired. What if you're like me, which you aren't and I guarantee that, but for the moment say you were and if you were like me, you'd be good at killing people, for a living, that's if anyone would let you live doing what I do.

So, now that you're me, and you stop doing what you're good at, which is killing people, what happens to you? What would your or my firing entail? Well, now, we both know getting fired would probably include and I mean literally, getting fired.

Cute, isn't it?

I wake up to the taste of blood and the searing pain of my good old friend Macro-shock sending my muscles into seizure. I'm sitting in that chair, that unholy, unsightly, evil, crooked, stained, and cold chair. In front of me one retriever, behind me, to the left someone I can't see, but I know they're there, watching. I hear scratching, strange mechanical scratching, somewhere just behind me.

"Why didn't you execute Brandon Cain's policy?"

"Who?"

I play dumb, or rather, I play drugged and can't remember what I did yesterday even when I really do know what I did yesterday or rather, and more importantly, what I didn't do yesterday.

This time, unlike many times before, they don't wait. There isn't a pause to recharge, power, or my body. Instead, I'm greeted by brilliant current, striking every nerve like a chord on a badly tuned guitar, shivers.

When it stops, after several very painful reminding seconds, I gasp for air.

My torturer screams,

"Who are you?"

I respond, "Greyor Allblack."

"And what do you do?"

Robotically I rehearse my purpose.

"When given a policy I find an appropriate way to execute it by instruction or creative interpretation to best serve the terms of contract."

That means, in most cases, I make deaths look like accidents. That ensures the policies get fulfilled and everyone gets paid.

"Why didn't you fill Mr. Cain's policy?"

"Who is Mr. Cain?"

A voice sharply cracks from behind me. It is the person I couldn't see and still can't even though he takes a few steps forward, standing just outside my peripherals.

"He's lying, increase the current."

How do they know I'm lying?

That scratching from before gets louder, like someone is taking a pen and running it back and forth across paper, shit, a polygraph?

"That machine doesn't work, especially if I'm being..."

I'm silenced as more current is pumped into my body, I lose feeling in my legs, and it gets harder to breathe as my body is tossed around. As if I'm trying to detach myself from the chair, bonds and all, but I'm doing nothing to help this. I can't see as my eyes again roll backward and I feel my teeth crush against each other, top to bottom.

All the while that scratching continues, so I focus on it, even though I'm losing consciousness and every second feels a little longer than the last, I hold on. The room is all but gone as is my sight and the pain is so constant I don't feel it as I once did. As I slip, something flashes inside my head, a memory, one I don't remember. Not just a single stream of thought but a slew of images. Things I don't recognize. People, places, faces, and all of them bring familiarity, a kind I can't know, warm and somehow comforting.

The current stops and my vision returns.

"What was that?"

I say it out loud.

The man I can't see now stands next to my surveyor, the one who calls me a liar, and I immediately recognize him.

"What was what Grey?"

Sketch stands smiling at me, scratching a pen up and down on a clipboard.

"Nothing. What did you want to know again?"

Sketch looks at the surveyor shaking his head in disbelief, he knows, and if he knows, then I'm in trouble.

I'm weak, so weak; it's hard to hold my head up to look at him.

"Grey, why didn't you finish Cain?"

"Did I not do something I was supposed to?"

Let me explain something quickly, whenever I fill a policy, successful or not I'm retrieved, doped, and I "forget." I'm supposed to retain memory during the policy, but nothing after, or before. Obviously, this process works, maybe not for me, but it works for others, others like me. Now, I'm not saying I remember everything because I don't, but I do remember everything since I started here.

My thoughts interrupted by a clipboard smashed against my face.

"Grey, pay attention! Why didn't you fill Cain's policy? You're really falling behind in your work."

What is he talking about? Falling behind?

"I don't know." I blurt out without thinking.

"You don't know?"

Sketch looks up at the surveyor, looks at me, and then back to him.

"Greyor, how do you feel? Have you been feeling different lately?"

The surveyor speaks up, flashing a pen light in my eyes.

"I'm having trouble remembering."

"That is just a side effect. Anything else? Emotions you don't recognize? Pain without wounds?"

"No."

"Alright Greyor, you let us know if anything changes, we are going to increase your medication."

Something unfamiliar, a voice, or more like a forced thought shatters into my subconscious,

"Don't do this."

"Why?"

I chirp out finding the strength to look through the light and at him.

"Your injury is causing complications."

"Injury?"

I feel a sharp pain in my neck as Sketch stabs me with something, almost instantly after he removes it, I'm out.

Don't let them do this to you, the more you take, the more you'll lose.

A voice, somewhere deep in my thoughts, rings of familiarity—from where, I don't know—but I know it. I'm unconscious and I see only dark. Whatever I was injected with synthetically lulls me, but doesn't remove some realm of consciousness, because somehow, I can hear outside of my current state. I can hear Sketch and the retriever.

"Why does he remember?"

"I don't know... it doesn't make sense."

"Does Henry know about this?"

Who the fuck is Henry?

"I don't know either, but he should know, and he should know soon."

"Increase his dosage, take him back to his room, and then let Henry know. As soon as you know anything, I better be the first to know, get me?"

"Yes sir."

I feel someone lean in close to me. I can feel their breath on my ear, and I can smell the rank of it. "I hope for your sake Grey, you don't remember."

MIDNIGHT

I wake to the sound of my own screams. Stirred from a dream I can't remember and left with a feeling I can't understand. Every night at midnight, without fail, I wake. I can never remember this dream no matter how hard I try. This dream brings the same pain, the same sickness, night after night. I don't understand what exactly causes this and I recognize it is just a dream, but the feeling it leaves stays even when the dream is over.

It feels as if something has been taken from me, something deep in me feels empty, as if someone ripped it from my ribcage as I slept. It is pain, insurmountable. I can't figure out what it is, but I want it gone, and now. I grab my heart, pulling at the flesh, expecting it to move from its fixed place on my chest. I have salty tears stinging my cheeks and running into my mouth.

I sit completely up, pulling my legs from under the sheets and letting them hang off the bed. I stare at the wall. The bare, almost white, and teal paint that seems colorless but as you stare you see the somewhat aquamarine stain, badly painted over the white. My room, only big enough for this tiny bed, sink, toilet, me and the horrible dead bolt door that separates me from a would-be endless hall that I've never walked alone. There is an electronic mechanism that requires a key card on the other side of the door, at about waist level, on the right. I've witnessed them swipe their card from both sides of the door, before they get me, and when they put me back. This is my cage.

I distract myself by focusing on something else, on the drag marks, the small dots of my blood leading me back to my bed. I remember them, and when they happened. But the pain, the pain doesn't go away. Like something opening up, hungry, and never filling. It hurts but it isn't something I can ignore like I do most of the pain I endure regularly, this comes and passes on its own. I don't even know what it is or what to call it, even if I did know those things, would it make it hurt any less?

I'm disoriented from waking too quickly and confused by what I feel. It is familiar and foreign all rolled into one, shoved, and buried inside my chest. It is localized to my chest, near my heart, next to it, or even behind it. This is mental, not physical, I don't know how I know, but, I'm sure. It is just in my head. It dries my mouth, so I go to the sink to take a drink, and I lean my head under the faucet as it spews cold water.

I take gulp after gulp as if I'm trying to fill that emptiness or maybe, even better, drown it. I drink till I can't breathe. Finally, when I've had my fill, I throw water on my face. As I rise, time seems to slow, my mind unprepared for what I'm about to see: my reflection.

This mirror hadn't been there before, or maybe it had, and I never looked. I can't remember which one it is and if it matters or not, but I feel like it does. Something so simple.

Look at yourself.

My eyes don't leave the faucet. I don't look in the mirror. I don't want to – even though I do. I go to the bed instead, and sit there, soaked in my sweat. I look up to a corner of my room, where both walls meet, left of the door. There is a camera. It is small and black and can rotate to capture the entire room, under the lens is a small red light signifying someone is watching. Next to the camera is a speaker- I can hear the buzz of it – like someone has the finger on the button about to bark orders at me but it just hums away.

I can hear whispering; maybe talking, but the thick walls make it sound like whispering. I can't decipher what is being said or how many are talking but it is coming from behind my bed.

The pain transcends my focus as I'm torn from whispering. It forces me to appreciate the agony I don't know.

Remember

I shake my head, growing dizzy from tossing it left

to right. I look up at the small plate-glass window on my door, waiting for a shape to overtake the darkness of the hallway. I sit there for several minutes—maybe more because my concept of time is malfunctioning— no one comes. I look up at the camera, my pupils flash from the plate-glass portal to the empty lens, so quickly that I beat the frame rate and it probably looked as my eyes never left the door.

Another wave of searing agony as my face twists from blank to expression. My forehead wrinkles. My eyes squint. My dimples pull downward, and I clench my teeth as fresh tears spill across my cheeks. I close my eyes,

I see sunlight and feel comfort as I roll on what I can only describe as a pillow top. I'm on a mattress, snuggled in sheets, and next to me— better yet— pressed up against me is a body. I breathe in deeply, aroma fills my nostrils, opening them as I suck down the smell, down to the bottom of my lungs. My eyes adjust as I stare at blinds – the black-out kind, the kind that keeps the sun off you when you sleep. They project little lines of light on the puffy grey carpet beneath the bed. I roll over and I'm greeted by long beautiful silk that sticks to my face. Her hair catches my stubble and I'm overwhelmed by the smell. I wrap my hands around her waist and pull her body into mine. She moans and nestles against me.

"Good morning baby." She whispers.

My eyes open, because I hear the lock disengage, and they are now focused back on the big door with the plate-glass window. Just outside it, two – maybe three people wait for the door to open.

I was right. Two enter, one waits outside, and I don't know who it is. Likewise, I don't know either one who enters my cage.

"Get up."

I stand, slowly, lurching to a stand.

"Turn around."

"Why?"

They look at each other. Then in unison, they look back at me.

"Turn around."

I turn slowly, extending my back, humoring their request.

They move forward at the same time, harmonized, as if they practiced this over and over until they got it right. Each reach for me, greeting my wrists with large metal cuffs, abrasive steel bonds much larger than police issued handcuffs. They lock with a mechanical beep.

"Turn around."

I turn and face them. Both stand a foot from me. Same attire, same haircut, hair color, eye color and exactly the same height – they are twins. I express my unease with a shudder as they extend their hands, pointing at the door, and they do it at the exact same moment.

"Creepy. Do you guys practice that?"

I walk through the door, and they stay right behind me, always a foot away.

Out into the massive hallway, greeted by the third, and thankfully he looks nothing like these two.

"Hello Greyor."

I look at this man. He's small, under average height, his hair pulled back by wax. His eyes are beady behind darkened glasses. He has a long lab coat on, open slightly exposing a polyurethane jacket, under that a white shirt, and his pants are black dress slacks that may or may not be too big for him.

"My name is Hanson; do you remember me?"

I look back at the twins, who stare out past me, uninvolved in this moment, and they look like they're waiting for something.

"Nope, should I?" I say, slightly smirking.

"I guess not, I know you, but I can't recall if we have been introduced prior to this - funny thing about memory. Please, follow me."

He turns and walks down the-would be-endless hallway, even though I know it ends, or should I say, turns into a different corridor. I try to count the number of doors – I get to twenty-two. I turn quick, glancing at my number. My room is sixteen. Each door is separated by faded teal walls and every door—like mine—has plated-glass windows and dead-bolt mechanically sealed doors, all but one door. That door doesn't have a plate-glass window, you can't see inside, and now my curiosity runs wild.

"Who is in that room?"

Hanson doesn't stop, respond, or acknowledge my question so I don't bother asking. I just look back, down toward my room, and then my gaze goes to the robots who are so close I could smell their breath. That is if they were breathing normally, and when I say normally, I mean at least appear to breathe but they don't. They also don't even recognize I'm looking at them.

Several turns, right around one, and left around another and now I know where we're going.

The interrogation room, my interrogation room. Hanson opens the door with his card, beep, and we all walk in. The room is different, the chair isn't there, the macro-shock machine isn't there. Things have been moved around and replaced by other machines.

The twins escort me to a machine, it is a scale, mechanical, but it is a scale. Hanson moves off to the machines, standing alone, he flips a switch, a hum and then a buzz begins.

"Please stand still Greyor."

He presses something and my shackles come off, one of the twins picks them up and then they both stand back.

The scale is a circular metal disk, from beneath the disk a large piece of what looks like metal extends from the floor to almost the ceiling.

"One hundred eighty-five point ninety-two centimeters tall. Seventy-five point seventy kilograms."

He nods and a moment later the door we came in opens and a girl in white carrying a tray comes in. She walks toward me, subtly swaying. She is wearing an almost white candy-striper shirt and a pencil skirt. Her blonde hair is pulled back into a tight ponytail, her green eyes glazed over, and she looks like the twins – expressionless and necrotic. She extends the tray; on it, my pills and a small cup of water.

They increased the dosage, don't take them.

I grab the pills and toss them into my mouth, with a hard swallow, and a gulp from the miniature glass I wash them down. I look at Hanson, who is blatantly staring at the nurses' ass. I look at the twins, who look out past me, at nothing. I look to where they are looking, but I can't seem to find what they're focusing on, if anything.

Hanson shakes his head as she leaves and then looks at me, and he almost looks embarrassed as he now realizes I've been watching him, but from my expression, I resemble the twins and the nurse.

"Alright Greyor, please step off the scale."

I do.

"How do you feel?"

"Fine."

"You've been struggling, haven't you? You look tired."

"I'm fine."

"You can talk to me Greyor, I'm your friend."

No, he isn't.

"I am fine."

"Alright Greyor – well, if you feel strange at all, let me know. These pills should help. You'll be back to normal in no time."

"What do you mean normal?"

"Of course, Greyor, you have brain damage. Whether you remember this conversation or not, I don't mind explaining it again. You had an accident..."

"What accident?"

"An accident Greyor, and in time, we will help you remember."

I try to remember, but I can't, and it makes me sick to try.

"You have blocked the memories Greyor, not on purpose of course but the trauma caused you to forget. We are testing the right dosage to help you remember."

He talks to me like I'm a child, like I don't remember what I do, as if he thinks I don't remember that I've been killing people – which is good, because I want him to keep thinking that.

"Greyor, slowly things will come back, but I need you to try. I want you to think about how you feel when you first take the medication, remember the first effects – focus on them. In time, with your help, and the help of the pills we'll be able to find the triggers to your memory and discover how to fix you."

Lies, lies, and more lies. He knows what they do to me. I want to lash out and snap his neck, but I know I wouldn't get far.

Why did you take the pills?

I know the intention of these pills. Too erase memory, long or short, it doesn't matter and I'm not going to try to understand how it works or how it is intended too. I just want to stay alive. I know if they knew, then I'd be dead, just like Sketch said—he hopes I don't remember.

Well, somehow, I hope I do.

While I've been thinking, Hanson continues lying, and it makes me wonder if I have any allies here, in this place, wherever this place is. I never know how I get back here, I always wake up here, and if I can change that I will.

Not if you keep taking every dose, they give you.

I get dizzy suddenly. I fall, and the twins catch me.

"Take him back to his room. He needs to sleep."

They drag me out of the room, and I welcome it because that room was spinning too quickly for me to stand.

Hold on, don't let go yet.

Too late, my head slumps over, and I'm gone.

ALEXANDER BURISH

Sometimes policies require time. In this case, my next policy, Alexander Burish, required three days - no more and no less.

Alexander worked for a privatized security firm. That week, he and his company were to escort diplomats to and from the airport. They used black GMCs with two percent window tint, each pane probably constructed from polycarbonate thermoplastic, otherwise known as bullet-resistant glass. It can be anywhere from seven to seventy millimeters thick. Each door is equipped with ballistic steel plates. There are probably other modifications like an explosion-resistant fuel tank, remote starter for the car, pressure and temperature control of the self-inflating tires, a siren or maybe an alarm, an intercom between the exterior and interior of the car, and a PA system. Maybe the inside is sealed or over-pressured, using its own air supply, to protect against poison gas or tear gas attacks. It all depends on how much money his firm invests to protect their clients.

No matter, because either way, I prepared for this situation. Let me start by saying something about preparedness. It doesn't matter how well you plan something, nothing, and I mean nothing, ever goes the way you plan it. This is common knowledge. Now, in saying that I don't mean that you should never prepare because it is a start for when you have to change plans - you have a foundation, something to work off, like I did.

Day one.

Alexander—I will call him Alex—leaves his condo at quarter to seven. I'm across the street going over the files on my phone, sitting at a bus stop on a wooden bench; the bench is held together by green spray-painted iron. He gets into his Tahoe and leaves his street. I wait several minutes before the bus shows up. I get on and head to the back walking past the regal blue seats bordered by polished steel. Every several feet, bars snake up, to hold on to, in case no seats are available. At the front of the bus is a bench seat on either side, those seats are for the elderly and disabled, putting them close to the front exit of the bus. I head to the back, past the back exit and up a small two step staircase to the similar looking bench with the same regal blue and steel seats.

This bus takes twelve minutes to get to the central bus station, which is situated in the core of the city bordering the transit-way. The station is on an island with two sides for buses going in opposite directions. The structure is glass and red metal; it is cold despite the transit owner's intention to warm the place up with color. It is just metal, glass, and concrete with red paint. They are stops for different buses and the buses head west, east, and south. I'm waiting for the bus that takes the transit-way all the way to the airport.

I can smell stale beer, urine, and cigarette smoke. A couple feet away, a guy stands puffing on a cigarette, leaning up against a brown lamppost and on the lamp post there is a sign that clearly signifies no smoking. I smile, turning back, looking for the bus I need. I need to time this correctly, compensate for the bus being early or late, because since I've started taking them, there hasn't been one I've waited for that has been on time or anywhere near it - always early or late, never on time.

As that thought ends, I look over to see the bus snake around the terminal heading my way. I dig into my pockets and find my bus tickets. I pull the neon blue cardboard sheets that will allow me entrance and journey for maybe an hour and a half, depending on the time of the transfer. I walk up, mixing in with the large crowd that waits for the double doors to open. As they do, the bus driver yells,

"Step back."

I hear a beeping noise as the hydraulics lower the bus and a different beep as what appears to be a small metal drawbridge reaches out and connects the bus entrance to the curb. An old obese woman in an automated wheelchair zips out shouting, "excuse me," in a hoarse, rude, and guttural tone that spews up, choking through her throat like the sentence is hard to say or she is just so tired of saying it. As the crowd parts and I'm left wondering if she is in that because she's paralyzed or she's just too fat to walk. When the line gets to me, I smile as I place the tickets in a small slot that sucks them away within a second, I look at the bus driver who pays me no attention and with another smile I say,

"Transfer please."

She presses a button and out of another slot a thin sheet of paper drops out and before my hand is even there it is falling, I snap my hand out quick and lift it from the air before it even gets in a float. With that I have the bus driver's attention, she smiles at me and speaks,

"Good reflexes."

I nod and walk to the back of the bus; I can feel her eyes follow me and to confirm that feeling, I look at the glass of the bus and there in the reflection, my feeling is confirmed. When I walk through the innards of this metallic snake, past all the yellow bars, royal blue felt covered seats, and the half-way mark is a grey plastic polymer latex accordion membrane that expands and retracts after every turn. In the middle of that are two bench seats that spin on the carousel during those turns. I walk up the little set of stairs by the back door, which is the final of three double doors on this bus. I want to be on the driver's side between the three rows of seats, the window seat. This seat I need will be the seat I take every time I get on this bus in the next three days. A girl, mid-twenties, blonde and plump, is already in my seat. I slide up next to her and stare straight ahead. I feel her eyes on me, I feel her expression. She is obviously uncomfortable because in all the seats available, I took the one next to her.

I slide my phone open quickly, check the time, slide it closed, and begin to calculate and compensate for a late bus. I can make this work. As the bus passes station after station, I watch from the window. My focus is the road; the time between stops and I count everyone. Things are simplified by the driver calling out each stop and I remember every name.

"Excuse me."

The girl next to me breaks my inner dialogue, my focus. I look at her, smirking. She goes to stand as I slide to let her out of the seat before quickly retaking it. She reburies the earphones that she took out to inform me to move. I saw her pull the string for the next stop, but she doesn't know that. When her hands slip on the yellow bars that border the double doors to her exit, waiting to push them open to leave, she glances over her shoulder to give me a last look. Her eyes meet mine for a brief second and I flash her a warm smirk and she blushes rose. She walks out and heads wherever she's going, looking back before the bus is gone, but my focus has changed even when I can still see her from my peripherals.

The bus picks up speed heading toward an underpass. After that underpass there are only two terminals before it crosses a main road to take the airport parkway. I have my time, my average time between stops, compensating for schedule and number of stops, and distance between them. I have my numbers, but now I need to know when and how many times Alexander and his detail make this trip.

I wait until the bus stops at the very last terminal, before the bus disappears and changes from the transitway to the parkway. I get off and stand at the very end of the terminal, watching buses and people come and go. Luckily, I don't have to wait long before Alexander's detail comes up from the parkway, three GMCs strong, driving within one car distance from each other. I record this time and patiently wait for their return trip. In under an hour they return, flying by me, down the transitway and back on to the parkway.

They make this trip two more times both ways. I have my numbers. Tomorrow, I will know which truck he is in. I walk through the station, down cold green-tinted concrete stairs, through the underpass and then back up cold concrete stairs and out on to the other side of the terminal so I can bus back. I add these factors in, how long it takes me to get across terminals, maybe this will help with my exit; I don`t doubt that when I make my move. I will only have a very small exit window; plan or no plan, killing someone in broad day light leaves very little room for error. Room or windows, this is going to happen regardless. When the bus finally gets here, I relax. My first day, despite being long, has rewarded me with the knowledge I came for. Tomorrow, I'll be at the airport waiting for Alexander`s detail. The transit system and the airport at least have one thing in common: the turn-over rate of people is insurmountable. The likelihood anyone will remember is a mathematical inconsistency, even if you go through there every day, the most recognition you'll get is familiarity, as though someone may say,

"Haven't I seen you somewhere before?"

If you hear that line, doing what I'm doing, you better cease to do what I do because you're doing it wrong.

Don't get noticed.

Day two:

The thing about public transit is you have numerous strangers riding the same bus, some going the same place, some going completely different places. Everyone is in their own little world, even the bus driver. Most have very monotonous patterns, daily rituals; same bus, same day, every day. Every single day. Sometimes the exact same people even. Going wherever they are going, knowing nothing about the person sitting a foot away, sitting right next to them. This is the portrait of this generation, whether intentional or not. People are oblivious to things happening; sometimes they are so oblivious they don't notice things happening right next to them.

My new regiment of medication, the new dose, has me focused but groggy. I try to sit up straight peering down past the back of people's heads. I count the number of people, notice who is here, who I saw yesterday. The bus flies down the transit in the dark, I left my hotel earlier today than I did yesterday. The morning is cold and dark. I am amongst the early risers, the ones who rise to the dark and fall to the dark. Poetic or not, that is exactly what it is like, and it feels off. Some will go to their halogen filled cubicles and pray time will fly but it doesn't. I can see it in their expressions; these people don't want to go where they are going. I look to my reflection but before my eyes meet the glass, someone sits down next to me. I turn slightly to look but instead of meeting their gaze I look on. The scenery is wet asphalt and concrete barriers. Out of a tunnel and past a terminal we cross a bridge. This is the first thing I can see through the semi-fogged window. Out of the window I see a river snake between shore to shore with heavy willow trees hanging into it. Endlessly, it runs toward a black back drop with a small orb of fire cutting up through the pink and burning out the grey.

I know that river; I just don't remember its name.

This bridge is right before the core bus terminal. We pull through it but today I don't have to transfer buses. This bus will take me all the way to the airport. I try to catch sight of that river and see that image one last time, but it is already out of sight.

This airport consists of three levels; the ground is for the arrivals: local and international, baggage transfer, ground transportation, rental cars, parking, shops, and finally a chapel. The second floor is gates, express check-in with no baggage, more parking, shops, and restaurants. The third and final floor is express check-in with baggage, US check-in and gates, US baggage transfer, even more shops and restaurants, and finally: the observation deck.

From the observation deck on the third level, I can see straight out to the private hangers and there I can see which GMC Alex will be in. I grab the escalator on the main level; I get to the second floor and have to walk to get a different escalator to the third level. I walk amongst people, some running, some walking, and just like the transit system, they're all going different places. Past security, past baggage handlers, help desks, shops, and more shops I make my way to the observation deck, which is on the other-side of a small restaurant.

I walk up, flush against the glass looking out across the entire terminal, and I watch the hustle and bustle of airline workers, motorized baggage carriers, loading bays, and wing walkers walking next to moving aerial monsters made of aluminum preparing their pre-flight procedure.

I smile and begin to take pictures, snapping shot after shot, but the direction of my camera is not pointed at what I appear to be watching; no, it's pointed at a hanger far west of the main terminal. At the terminal, half a dozen men, maybe more, stand at the hanger doors waiting for a plane to land. However, no plane will land; this is further preparation for tomorrow. I snap photo after photo, leaving about thirty seconds between each shot. I capture frame by frame of Alex and his detail readying to move to the vehicles, and as they split into three teams, each team to take a GMC, I have him. Clowns to the left of him, jokers to the right, Alex is stuck in the middle GMC, back right seat with one other – the fake diplomat. Alex will be in the middle GMC, back right seat, protecting the diplomat.

I put my camera away and turn following the same

path to the exit as how I entered. I have one more thing to do to prepare for tomorrow. My only problem is the bullet resistant glass, if there is any. The standard .45 round won't have enough force to penetrate in one shot, not even several shots, maybe not even at all with an entire clip. Depending on the glass thickness and what it was made to withstand. Even then, most tests allow stability with bullet placement at a hundred and twenty millimetres of each shot. Unless I were to hit the exact same place several times and hope that the bullets penetrate the glass, and if one makes it through, kills Alex.

The required marksmanship to hit the same spot is difficult. Now, factor in that I'll be in one moving vehicle, he'll be in another vehicle moving the opposite direction - and I have to hide the fact I'm shooting from a bus and make sure not to let any of my casings hit anyone or simply fall to be collected for evidence. This makes it nearly impossible, I say nearly because nearly anything is possible, but this is highly improbable that I'll be able to do this and not be seen, let alone be successful in killing him. I have the right ammunition for the job, but it is the factors that keep the improbability of succession, and I have no room for error, but no time to make sure.

The right ammunition; I'll focus on that for now. When I get back to my hotel, I go to my trunk, and lift the trunk floor, accessing where one would normally keep a spare tire. Where my spare tire should be, there is a flat black metallic case. I go to my hotel room. Sit on the bed and leave the case on my lap. From it I pull my gun, my M1911A1 .45 magazine-fed, semi-automatic, recoil-operated, single-action handgun. I stare at it and recognize what it deserves; respect and nothing but. I can only imagine what this gun has seen before me, if a gun could see. This gun has a story, long before me, and I'll tell it later. Right now, I have to load it. The bullets I have for this situation I don't recommend using on anyone without body armour—I mean, gun shots aren't pretty, regardless—but these are unnecessarily nasty.

I take the box of bullets out, remove seven, and let them roll in my palm. These bullets are made especially for penetrating power. They don't deflagrate like normal ammunition. They are not hollow-point; they won't mushroom on impact, for greater wound cavity. These bullets are called HARPP, which is short for: hardened armour penetration priority. Normally, you don't see .45 caliber versions of hardened armour penetration priority, but then again, what I do is far from normal. Sometimes the tools needed are different, but they usually get the job done. They should get the job done.

I can't use hope. I can't use chance. They will get

the job done.

Bullet proof doesn't exist. There is bullet resistant. That is why it's called bullet resistant glass. After awhile you can penetrate anything. The laws of thermodynamics have yet to be proven wrong. Everything created can be destroyed. Anything built can be disassembled. Nothing physical is invincible.

I spin the suppressor on to the end of the barrel—I still haven't quite figured out the distraction I need—because I know, when I start firing, someone will notice.

Tomorrow will prove if people are actually oblivious to things happening a foot away. So, whomever the unlucky person sitting next to me tomorrow might be—I hope for their sake—they are as, if not more, oblivious then everyone a foot away from them.

I feel my tongue dry. I put my gun down and walk to the washroom. I leave the light off and I turn the tap on. Run the cold water and wait. I stand there motionless in the dark. I can see my reflection cast in the mirror just above my eye sight.

Look.

I ignore that little voice. I go into my pocket and search for my medication. I pull the medication bottle out. The saffron bottle with a single white sticker wrapping around its circumference and on that single white sticker is a code. My pills have a code. Specific only in the last few digits and those digits are mine. I rub the label with my thumb. Over and over until part of it hangs off. I look up at that mirror and in the dark I see my silhouette. No details, only shadow and the shapes behind me. The toilet and shower, its curtains and the little towels hanging on the towel rack. The yellow light from the lamp in the bedroom just gives me enough light to see my eyes.

I pop the ivory lid of the saffron bottle and pour two pills into my hand. They look bigger.

Don't.

I throw them into my mouth and stand up in front of the sink. I lean down, dodging the snaking faucet, and drink down large gulps of freezing water. I feel the pills sink down my oesophagus. I turn the tap off and walk back over to the bed. Clearing it carefully, I neatly place my gun back in the case. I close the box of bullets and put them back in the case. I turn off the light and I lie down in the dark, still in my clothes, staring up at the ceiling fan that spins round and round and round. I can now hear it, something I didn't give any attention to before, but with each oscillation I'm captured by it, and now all of my focus is on the ceiling fan.

I don't usually take my medication in the middle of a job given that it is supposed to help me forget, but I've been feeling distracted. Distracted by details,

details that aren't fact, and me giving them this much focus will result in an issue I don't need. What I have is Alex and what route he takes, which GMC he will be in, and where to hit with enough time to disappear when they realize Alex has been hit and not who they are protecting. As I said early, risk results in reward when it comes to the policy. Sure, you pay more into it, but my company pays out for it. Then again, Alex has no idea that he is going to die tomorrow, and he never would expect it would be from the same people who insured his life.

I sit up. Slowly, my eyes crawl to that ceiling fan that buzzes overhead. Whooshing around and around, each rotation looks the same, and it simply looks still as though it's not moving, when I know it is; a simple optical effect.

I understand this effect, I understand this ceiling fan. My memories are like that fan; it looks like I'm not remembering, feels like not remembering, when in fact, I am, and it is distracting. For the moment, despite how difficult it is, I need to leave that door closed. I can't focus on those thoughts now. I start to sweat, start to feel sick, and the room begins to spin like that fan overhead. I feel like I'm having a bad reaction to the medication.

Maybe, I shouldn't have taken them.

Too late for that, let it happen, remember.

I slowly lay back and I focus all of my attention, every single bit on that fan, and how it spins round and round. I close my eyes and just listen to the fan. I feel as if I'm about to be sick, something rushing up from inside me quickly. It isn't vomit. No, it feels like I'm falling unconscious. As though even with my eyes closed the darkness just gets darker and not like when you try and squeeze out light with your lids. More like that moment right before you fall asleep; when you recognize you are about to fall asleep. Whatever this is; coming quickly, let me guarantee you, it is not sleep. It is something else.

Am I dreaming this?

I shake it, open my eyes and sit up, but I can't sit up because I'm already standing. The hotel room is gone, and it is replaced by forestry.

What the fuck?

I'm in a forest. How the hell did I get here?

Shut up and watch.

I see a black shirt, hanging on a tree, it moves so slightly, so subtly in the wind. Suddenly, a gunshot, and then the shirt has a cavity in it. A .38 caliber opened this cavity, mid torso, low abdomen. I follow the trajectory of the shot, and I see a man standing past the tree line on the shore of a creek, just at the top before it falls into the sand bank. He seems angry and confused, he seems like he thought he was shooting someone. This all feels like its slow motion, the damage to the shirt, the reaction of the shooter and I'm watching from next to the tree that just got shot but the man doesn't recognize my existence. He slowly turns his attention, his face freeze frames, each blink of his eye I get to watch open and close, and an expression slowly creeps over his face and that expression is surprise.

I'm already looking at what he is trying too.

A shirtless man, young, maybe eighteen to twenty with long feathered brown hair, tanned from the sun, wearing tight dark blue denim jeans, is charging from a crouched position right near him. He springs from the ground and spears into the shooter. He connects with his ribs and his arms wrap around his torso. They both fly from the bank and fall toward the creek. I watch the hit change his expression. I see the .38 caliber pistol in his hand fly free from his grasp as they fall and when that happens, time speeds up. When it hits the ground, I move to the bank where they stood so I can watch this.

I get there just in time to see them both surface from the water. Before the shooter can get to his feet, he catches a solid hit in the right cheek and staggers, but before he can recover, the shirtless guy hits him again and again. In a daze, the shooter swings once. The shirtless guy dodges that and throws a hit into his ribs. The shooter stumbles back. When the shooter goes to punch him again, the shirtless guy ducks and shifts behind him, and this is when I see the blade. The shirtless guy removes a long serrated knife from a sheath on his belt. Spinning it in place and as soon as it is firmly in his grasp; he plunges it and buries the blade to the hilt in this guy's lumbar vertebrae, as he wraps his arm around the shooters punching arm and throat. One fluent motion has this shooter in a choke hold and a knife lodged deeply in his lumbar vertebrae. Viscous crimson spills over this guy's hand as he twists the knife, and the shooter struggles less and less until the shooter stops completely.

He is really good with a knife.

When he goes limp, the shirtless guy releases him and watches him hit the water. The shirtless guy takes several steps back and then looks up at me. He doesn't see me, he just stares past me. I watch every accelerated breath, I watch his chest rise and fall in close repetition. I watch those repetitions grow farther and farther apart. I know that feeling. That is adrenaline coursing through him violently and his body is compensating to slow it down. He stands there, slowly his breathing normalizes. He freezes as he looks at his hands, watching the droplets of blood run between his fingers. He dunks his hand in the water, removes it, rubbing his other hand, trying to wash the blood, but it just runs now on both hands.

Do you remember?

Day three,

I hear an alarm, annoyingly pulsing over and over again from outside of this. My eyes click open, and I turn my head to see the time. Fuck, I overslept. I spring from the bed and hit the washroom. I throw the tap on and before I throw water on my face, I see my medication bottle hanging on the edge of the sink, empty.

What the fuck? All of the pills absent from the saffron bottle with no sign of exit. None stray on the counter or the floor. They are gone. This isn't good, how do I even explain this? I don't have time for this right now; I'll deal with it later. I throw hot water in my face; it burns my cheeks and runs down my face warming me to complete consciousness. I swing the tap off and stumble into the bedroom; I notice that the fan is off. I look around for my case, which is on the table, open. My gun is in pieces, properly disassembled into each piece. I sit down at the desk.

Are you kidding me?

I have to put this back together again. I slide the barrel assembly back together. The recoil spring guides inward and the curved bottom rests against the barrel. Holding the recoil spring guide, I slide it onto the frame rail. Pulling the slide back until the rear, small, circular notch in the slide aligns with the rear slide hole. I align everything so that the rear, small, circular notch and the rear slide stop hole are in place, and I also make sure the alignment for the slide stop pin hole and barrel linkage hole are correct. Pressing the slide stop, I compress the plunger and hear the snap telling me it is in place. I cycle the slide to make sure the barrel stays in place and does not move. I move the slide forward and insert the barrel bushing rotating it clock wise all the way in. I insert the recoil spring and then compress the recoil spring and recoil spring plug. I hold the recoil spring plug down, rotating the barrel bushing counter-clockwise until I feel the bushing lock and the recoil spring plug is in place. I slide the assembly open, cycling it to ensure it is ready to use, and it is. Finally, I thread the suppressor, and my gun is ready again.

I check the clip, making sure the right ammunition is still in it, before feeding it back in. I throw on the safety and slide it into the laptop bag I've chosen to capture expended rounds. I look around, double checking before leaving my room and heading out. I want to make sure nothing else is off, or misplaced, and somehow, I have to distract myself from trying to figure out what happened.

I'm back on the bus, headed toward the main terminal. I need to change buses and grab my seat. This isn't how I planned things to happen, but like I said, few things ever go as planned. At the terminal I wait for my bus. I wait with strangers and with people I've seen over the last two days. I turn my attention on those I've seen. Eight people make the same trip, day in and day out, or at least they have for the last three days. Out of these eight people, two stand out, one man and one woman and I say they stand out because they appear to actually enjoy riding the bus day in and day out. Appearances can be deceiving however, but I believe their emotion to be genuine and I doubt it is about riding the bus, rather they enjoy each other's company.

Again, this is only my observation, but I have a tendency to focus on details that extend from my observations and more often than not, they are correct.

Today—despite the oddity in how I woke— follows the past two days. Same people, same bus, same bus schedule, and how late the bus is. I factored this in, but my nerves have taken over; this may be the perfect opportunity to fill Alex's policy, and I don't want to miss it.

I see the bus I need to be on five minutes ago snake around the terminal. My tongue dries. I rally behind the herd and wait at the stop. It slides up, connecting to the curb. We wait patiently for the doors to open, no one pushes their way on, and finally, with a press of a button, they do. Everyone quickly gets on. Hurrying their way to their seats, as though that will make the bus arrive on time or get them where they had to be five minutes ago. I, unlike the rest, am in no hurry. I take my time. I smile at the bus driver, ask for a transfer, and begin to walk away. Then, suddenly, I stop myself mid isle and stand absolutely motionless as my answer comes to me.

I need a distraction. In order for this to work I have to make worlds collide; to get strangers interested in the same thing, at the same time; all together. I need to bring these people together and now I have my way. I turn and walk back to the bus driver, leaning over, I smile,

"Hey, long day?"

"You can say that again. Can I do something for you?"

"Maybe. You see that couple back there?"

I turn very casually and nod at the couple who enjoy their time together, the coworkers I've noticed the last several days. I remember glancing at his Id, his work Id, on it his name, and his name is Todd. Her name, what is her name? Think. Remember and I do. Her name is Nancy.

She looks in her isle mirror glancing as she starts the bus. As the bus moves forward, she looks up at me.

"Yeah, what about them?"

"Today is their anniversary, and Todd asked me to set something up and the only way I can do that is with your help. Todd wants to ask Nancy to marry him, but he wants you to announce it like it was a stop, instead of saying the stop, at three thirty four will you please ask Nancy if she will marry Todd?"

I smile, as if I'm sincere, as though Todd asked me to do this for him.

She looks at the road, she glances up at me, she looks back to her steering wheel and then she sighs.

"Sure, I'd be honoured. You better be the best man."

"I hope so."

I turn and walk toward the back. Past the glances of people who sit up in their royal blue, steel bordered row seats. Past the yellow bars that border their seats; down the isle of anti-slip grip flooring; through the middle grey flexing accordion that shivers with the inertia of the road and finally over the small stair case by the back door and into my window seat on the drivers-side of the bus, I place my bag on my lap and zip open one of the larger pockets. I slide my M1911A1 under my arm and rest my other hand on the small black knob that will open the sliding single piece frame window.

I watch the landscape fold into itself with the hues of concrete and bus terminal colors. All of the images meld next, one second it is a solid concrete overlay and then the next suddenly interrupted by forestry. Greens and browns separating the dead grey momentarily. Other buses fly by and in those buses, countless faces of strangers that phase away details with the speed of passing each other.

I adjust my posture. Correct my focus. Allow a new mode to take over. I'm vigilante in the attention of my surroundings but relaxed enough to avoid further attention. I pull the hammer of my gun back and ready. My other hand impatiently waits to slide the window open. I take a long, endless breath inward, and wait. My eyes flick to my watch and recognize at once how close Alex is and then—almost hypnotically—I hear the crackle of the intercom. The sweet voice of the driver begins to ask a question and everyone on the bus who has a shred of attention hears the question. The crowd collected from stops past roars with celebration. The thunder of their claps overtakes the sound of the bus tearing down the open transit-way. I see the headlights of the first GMC. The window comes open. I slowly begin to exhale as my suppressor barrel penetrates the cold rapid air outside. Aim, squeeze, and release all the air in my lungs as I watch the back window of the second GMC disappear in shards as round after round dissolves the window, frame, even the door and then finally the back seat passenger.

To my gapping surprise—no bullet resistant glass—and because of that my choice of ammunition falls into the classification of overkill. Alex never had a chance in hell to live through that, body armour or not.

The three GMCs simultaneously break, screeching a fog of thick opaque grey. Some of the security detail spring out surrounding the vehicles on all sides, assault rifles pointed out and at every radial direction awaiting further assault. When they check on the one, they're protecting they will realize he is—or I should say—should be fine. Alex, however, was dead when the first bullet tore through his body armour at center mass, shattering his rib cage and liquefying his lungs, the second struck him in the celiac plexus, boring out nerves, and the third gored his carotid artery – he was dead before the GMC stopped.

All the while the bus is still in chaos from the question and to my surprise, the cheering is silenced momentarily by one word,

"Yes!"

And then the cheering resumes more thunderous than before. I look at Todd who is completely shocked by what is going on as Nancy chokes him in a tight embrace, kissing his face over and over.

I safety my gun, dropping it in the laptop bag to join the spent casings. I stand, closing the zipper and walking to the back doors to wait for the next stop. I ring the bell, carefully and subtly hiding myself from celebration and attention.

I know the security detail will soon have an idea of the trajectory and they will come speeding down after this bus, or maybe they won't, but I'm not leaving that up to chance.

With these thoughts, tracing over what just happened, and trying to figure out how a security detail doesn't have bullet resistant glass on their vehicles, and furthermore how I prepared the ammunition to deal with that, I can't seem to dissuade myself from the warmth that creeps over me.

I watched a man disappear and to do it, I set something beautiful into motion. I helped two strangers recognize, or rather, admit feelings for each other – well, I assume the feelings are mutual. I look at Todd who aesthetically looks overjoyed by the situation as he returns the affection. Nancy is locked tightly in his embrace, pecking at his cheek, and smiling and thanking strangers who now surround them, asking them questions. The bus stops but these people still stay around, watching intently, listening, and continuing with the same congratulations.

Without realizing I'm staring at them, smiling.

It is beautiful, isn't it?

Todd smiles at the bus driver, he mimes a word, and the bus driver nods at my direction but when Todd gets a chance to turn and look at his would be best man, I'm gone.

I'm already climbing the terminal stairs, up and down the walkway, through another set of doors I am out and, on the street, joining a new group of strangers, disappearing into the crowd.

While walking amongst bystanders, my thoughts run wild. I think of Alex, and I feel something. For him, a stranger, a policy...

A human being.

It is my job, I have to, and it is what I do.

Wasn't always.

But it is now and why do I care about Nancy and Todd, they worked to be a perfect distraction.

Made you feel good, didn't it?

With that, I do, but at the same time, I don't. I struggle with what I just did to Alex. I'm unsure if I'm angry that I spent so much time preparing, worrying about the glass, about if my bullets would go through. Or is it because I just slaughtered him?

I'm at the mercy of emotions I haven't felt. Conflicted with what could be remorse and overwhelmed by pride for either the succession of filling Alexander's policy or helping two strangers recognize they do in fact just enjoy each other's company. I can't determine what is worse, losing control, or gaining comprehension because the company can't find this out, find out that I have a conscience, and it is bleeding out and distracting me from my work.

Don't let them.

Immediately, I jump from my inner dialogue and realize I'm standing in front of a store, flush against the glass, looking through my own reflection, and if I stand back only a step, I can see myself.

Look, do it, go on.

I don't move, however, because through the dark reflection I can see behind myself, just over my shoulders I see several men move through the crowd toward me. I know them. I know why they are here. Retrievers...

HELENA AIMES

I'm at the bottom of a lake looking up at the amorphous surface. Beyond it, Helena Aimes prepares to take what will be her final dive. She is a schoolteacher, a physical education teacher. She is a natural swimmer and from what I've seen, enjoys nothing more than being immersed in water. Every Saturday morning, she swims across this lake, from one shore to the other, and then returns to where she parked her car. Today, her husband is watching her kids, and they will wait patiently—just like they have before—wait for their wife and mother to come home from this swim, but today she will dive in, and she won't come out. Police divers will find her in a couple of days, or maybe by tonight, depending on how fast the police do their job.

That deep breath she is taking. That preparation to get a good start to what would be a vigorous, long swim, will be her very last breath because I'm going to take her life and any hope of future from her. Normally, she wouldn't have to be careful when diving in, because the bottom and all dangers are far below. But today, six feet and one inch plus my seventy-three-inch reach, with a large, jagged rock at its end, will insure she won't come up. The rock waits patiently in my hands. When she dives in, her skull will connect with it, and all I have to do is hold it above me.

This rock will take her consciousness, render her incapacitated, and she will drown. So, if this hasn't sunk in, all I'm going to do is simply lift the rock above my head and let gravity do the rest. This is yet another accident brought to you by Grim Associations, carried out by me. I watch her breath in; I know this breath, this cycle of air because I've seen her do it several times, enough to familiarize myself with her ritual. She is a creature of habit and because of this I'll know when to lift the stone. It is always about timing. If only she would look down and see me, she could prevent the inevitable. Then again, if she looked down, and saw me, it wouldn't be inevitable.

I stand motionless, shrouded by my dive suit, taking slow and small breaths in, actively trying to avoid agitating the water and warning her with bubbles. It is cold and still dark and translucent. Small rays of light cut through the surface and stop at a very exact point unable to penetrate the darkness below, they just glisten and reflect with the change of wind on the surface.

A piece of me wants her to see me, wants her to swear she saw something, to shake and rattle her just enough to instinctively know not to swim today, to go home and join her family. Then again, I could just leave the rock at my waist, cradled in my hands, swaying harmlessly in the water and not raise it as she dives in. She would clear me, swim on, and eventually tear triumphantly from the glassy prison sucking in sweet patient air before launching herself back under. Repeating this same thing until she reached the other shore and then repeat every step until she came back to where she left, and she would be alive. To feel alive; succeed at what she came to do. That feeling would last until next Saturday when she'd do it all over again.

A part of me recognizes this is exactly what should happen, for me to just witness and walk away, or swim away until I can walk away. By some selfish intrigue, some drive has me selfishly wondering where that leaves me. I came here to do this. By me walking away, I wouldn't get to do this again or anything again. They have made it clear, this is my purpose, and if I don't do it, if I don't kill Helena—or anyone I'm sent for—I lose my life.

What life? You think this is life? Do you not hear yourself? This isn't life.

That voice eats at me; my medication is far away, and I can't take it.

I know you hear me. Let go of the rock and walk away.

My fingers tense as I feel the weight of the stone— I've been holding it for a while—and as every minute passes, it gets heavier.

All I have to do is drop it, but if I do, Helena lives. Where does that leave me?

To do what you want. Drop the rock.

And if I do, where do I go... when I can't remember where I'm from? Where would I go where they couldn't retrieve me?

Remember. Drop the rock.

I can't. I look up at Helena and she is almost ready. Her ritual is almost complete.

Let the fucking rock go.

I came here to do this; if I don't do this, what use am I?

You're more. You'll be more. You aren't this. They made you this way. They don't want you to remember because you're so good at this. The only reason you do this is because you know nothing else, but you know nothing else because they took it from you. All you have to do is remember. Stop taking the medication and remember. You're drowning in those pills; you'll never get to be you, only the way they make you feel, and they make you not feel. So, you don't feel. The pills do. You can hide as much as you want, but eventually you'll take more and more just to feel nothing. And then? And then what? What do you keep locked away? I know you feel it, behind the mirror, scratching away. It'll keep going. Your identity intends to survive, and survival doesn't stop, especially when it is being threatened and the only way it is going to stop is if you let it out.

I remember nothing at all before this. I can't. I try. I wake up and I don't understand the things I feel, but I feel them, and they hurt. I don't know where it is from or what it is, but it makes this easier, doing what I do. I look back, to remember, and it isn't there. I only remember Southstone, Grim Associations, Sketch, Silk, doctors, nurses and...

And?

And who I've killed and how I've killed them.

That's not what they intended and that's not how this works. Whatever they are doing to you is temporary. If you can remember something. Anything at all. You can remember everything, but not if you keep doing this to yourself.

I'm not.

Yes, you are. Drop the fucking rock.

I can't.

Yes, you can.

I'm shaking. My breathing isn't controlled and because of that, small bubbles tremor upward, slowly ascending, teeter-tottering their way up. My shaking forces my balance slightly; I stumble subtly trying to balance, to gain a comfortable grip of the rock again. I look up at Helena, who's ready.

Look down. For fuck's sake, look down.

I tense my arms, my legs shake, and my body, in turn, quivers with the anticipation for what is next. Either that or I'm fighting to stop myself. That little part of me that doesn't want to do this grows and fights my hands, but I overwhelm that urge.

She takes several steps back. My arms begin to carry the rock upward, slowly, very slowly, and it ascends from my waist past my gut, up past my belly button, over my abs, up across my pectorals and past my face with my eyes staring, without blink or flutter, following it. She leaps into the air, cutting her frame into a crescent like she was mimicking the moon. She straightens out before breeching the surface. She has the grace and the strength of an Olympic diver.

My arms go from the bow positioning to straight, from bicep to elbow to forearm, until my wrists have the stone far above my head, blocking out the flickering light from above and darkening out the sun. She penetrates the water, flying toward the bottom. She begins to arch her path to submerge, and that collective force throws her into the rock, skull first. A small gash opens on her forehead, cutting from her left eyebrow right to where her hairline starts. A crimson jet of ink joins the water but seems to hang near the wound before moving and flowing incrementally away. Bit by bit, second by second, more blood seeps out.

I let her force the rock out of my hands after the initial impact. I watch the rock slowly waver as it sinks. I step back as she continues on with less motion than she started with. She goes limp as the cold overtakes her limbs and without conscious fight, she begins to sink. Motionless and statuesque, she descends, and I turn and watch her. It is almost majestic how still she is, even though moments ago she sped like a bullet tearing a path for a torrent trail behind.

As she reaches the lakebed, I think I see a shutter and I wait. Moments pass and nothing. She isn't moving. So, I kick from where I am and swim out across the lake toward the other side. I'll make her journey, but I won't swim back. I intend to exit the water how I entered it. From under the cover of large willows that break the shore and slowly sink into the water. From that cover, I'll exit the lake and get back to my car, or maybe they're waiting to retrieve me. Either way, I'm going back to Southstone.

Helena won't come out alone. Someone will pull her out. Today, tonight, or in a couple days, she'll be retrieved too.

I look back into the cloud of dust I kicked up as I make my exit through the darkness waiting beyond my hands. I can see her lifeless through the veil, waiting, and something inside me sinks.

Why didn't you just drop the rock?

For the same reason she didn't look down.

HOW I WAS MADE

I'm shivering and blind, I can feel the cold cut around me; reactively, I open my eyes. I look around, I see walls and windows. I'm standing in the mud in the middle of a courtyard. The grey walls of Southstone surround me and the brick glass windows squared out in their frames watch me, or someone behind them watches me. The ground is moist and covered in patches of dying grass. I'm naked under the hospital gown, its bleach white, thin fabric barely protecting my body and I have no idea, not even a realm of idea, how I got out here. This is the courtyard, the killing courtyard. I'm in the middle of it and I don't know how I got here. A buzzer is about to sound, and this is the first time, but not the last time, I'll hear it.

It goes off for three seconds and then three people spill out of the doors across the courtyard. They don't stop running; they run right toward me, and they are armed with asps. Two men and one woman.

I hear a voice; this is the first time I hear this voice and like the buzzer, and like the courtyard, it won't be the last time.

"They are going to kill you, Grey."

That's Sketch's voice. That rasp: this is his introduction. These people, I don't know them, but

Sketch is right, they want to kill me; they are colder than others I've seen here, as though something is off, something had been misplaced and left behind when they woke up today. They appear to have a complete lack of conscience, stripped of any and all humanity. It is confirmed they're missing something; I can see it in their eyes. When they get within five feet of me, and they fold forth the length of their asps, I stop thinking and start fighting for my life.

Is this what I'm supposed to act like? Look like?

All three strike in unison, almost hitting each other with little regard for comradery. I don't back up, I move into them, past them and their asps. I put myself right in the middle, grabbing one under his arm, moving my knee into his chest; I swing him quickly into the other, spinning. They topple down and before they recover, I side-step her swing, quickly grabbing her throat with one hand; I put my leg behind her and lift her head with my other hand by her chin, forcing her neck back. I keep her body straight, forcing one part back and keeping the rest of her solid. Her neck snaps back in my hands and with that, she's dead.

I release her, letting her free fall, and I turn to her recovered friends, who now swing ferociously, their intention is to cave in my skull. Intentions, I have none. My actions bring only results; they will die. Struggle or not, the result is always the same.

The first takes a shot at my body and I step back with a swing, wrenching him with me. He loses his balance, and the asp, which I recover without a moments waste. I bring it up to defend against a blow from the second guy. I push from that deflection and come down with my own strike that makes impact where elbow meets forearm. Even without emotion, I still see pain; you can't wash that away. I strike again and once more, before throwing my body into him. As he falls, I jump on him, positioning my knee with his throat, and when we hit the ground, I feel my knee sink, pushing his Adam's apple in. He chokes, struggling with the loss of air from his trachea, lodging itself deeply in his esophagus, completely restricting his airway.

I feel the cold metal of an asp on my throat as the final attacker is rearmed and sturdy behind me, pulling me back with one hand on each end of the asp, choking me. I dig my fingers between my throat and the asp, locking them around it.

With my left foot, I step firmly on his foot as he tries to wrench me backward. In turn, I push forward with my right foot and throw him over my back. He turns on to his back, but before he can stand, I'm already on him. I straddle his chest with my hips and when he strikes at me with the asp, I bring both my arms up, touching my hands to my head; with my elbows at a forty five degree angle, I take the blow. When he comes up for another strike, I punch down into his jaw. I lurch backward and punch down on his forearm that holds the asp. With another strike at me, I punch his wrist, and the asp flies out of his hand, toppling over my shoulder. I throw a fist back into his mouth and as his head swings back with the force of the hit, my hands go to his throat and I lift my body up and fall down with my knees on his chest, winding him. With that exhale, I force my hands down as hard as I can, and I begin to choke him. He limply strikes me; in the face, in the arms, he effortlessly smacks at me trying to break my grasp.

The will to survive exists in every living creature, in some more than others, but it is always there. You can't fight survival; you can't remove it. It'll always show, even when sometimes it is already too late. My survival instinct is very much dominant here, and elsewhere; I don't even know myself, but I know dying is the last thing I want to do, and of course it would be, it is the last thing anyone does. What I'm identifying is that I never even consider the situation; I just start protecting myself, blindly. I've already killed two people out here and there isn't a section left in me that will let this guy live. When he begins to gyrate, convulsing, and flailing, I tighten my grip. In desperation, he does everything he can to force me off, but I hold on. I choke every last breath from his body and even when he stops fighting, stops breathing, and he completely stops moving, I still hold on.

I let go finally, but it isn't because I know he is dead; it is because the buzzer goes off again. I stand quickly, turning every ounce of my attention to those doors. From the doors, a single man, casually saunters out, completely calm, almost strutting toward me. He is dressed in white scrubs, dirtied with blood splatter. He is roughly my height, heavier than me, with a shaved head and oceanic blue eyes. Just like his predecessors, he is expressionless. He stops about ten feet from me and studies me. He cracks his neck in a full circle and then, to my surprise, makes an attempt to smile.

Likewise, I'm expressionless. Deeply inhaling and slowly exhaling. Regaining my composure, I let my arms go limp. I feel cold again, but this time it is pleasant. Cooling me from my last encounter but quickly tightening my skin with its frigid touch. I'm again cold.

"Deshane. Kill Greyor."

As soon as Sketch finishes my name, Deshane is already in swing. I step out of the path of the heavy haymaker, but he is a lot quicker than he looks; as a left hook throws me off balance and before I can recover, he is on top of me, throwing me to the ground. We both hit the ground hard, but now I'm ready and I'm not getting pinned. When he comes down with a punch, I grab his arm, leading it into the ground. I slide out from under him to his side and throw my elbow into his cheekbone. With my other arm I bring it around his throat, but before I can get a tight grip, he throws his elbow into my ribs. I take the hit and roll back. I get to my feet just in time to see him fly toward me with another haymaker, with all of his weight behind it. I kick back, and as the fist flies by, I pull him into my haymaker. He gladly returns one to me, completely unaffected by my hit, while his feel like they're cracking bones. I stumble back as he quickly follows through with another, and another. I keep taking them and walking backward, trying to duck, and trying to weave, but Deshane has unwavering accuracy. I'm running out of distance. With every step backward, I'm so much closer to the wall, and I don't want to get cornered because with every hit, I taste more and more blood. Every hit feels as though it will permanently connect with my body, as if his fist buries beneath the blow. Every hit brings more and more pain. To make matters worse, he continues to strike the same three places, constantly switching the pattern so I can't learn his repetition; those three places are: my left eye, right side jaw, and nose. All of which are now swelling and splitting and bleeding.

When I defend one of his targets, he attacks another before I can react.

Remember what I said about survival instinct.

When my back hits the wall, his fist crushes my nose. Blood careens down my face, past my lips, and splatters on my gown, and on his scrubs. My arms go limp and I begin to slide down the wall. He grabs me by the throat with his left hand, lifting me to stand before burying his fist into my left eye. I see a flash of light from that blow. When he hits me in the jaw, my blood paints the wall. A huge stream spills from my mouth. He begins to pummel me. Continually, lifting me to my feet to endure another flurry of punches, and now I've lost feeling in my face. As he goes to bury his fist into my eye socket, taking a large step back, intending to render me unconscious with the entire weight of this haymaker, I open my right eye, and yes, I've learned his changing pattern – not like it matters now – he is about to go back to that original cycle which he does after mixing up the places he strikes after every three hits but he always returns to that original pattern. I know him and now this ends.

I spew a mouthful of blood in his face and sidestep that heavy hit which connects solidly with the wall behind me. The gun that is his fist shatters sickly, curling with a sick pop. As he cringes, he almost cradles into himself, like a fetus.

I quickly get behind him and boot him forward. He goes face first into the solid brick waiting a foot away. His face connects to the stone with the weight of my body behind him, and as he kisses it, his blood paints across its grey surface, decorating a square foot of it crimson, joining the splash I left with my blood. He buckles and falls to the ground. I jump on his back with my knees and grab his forehead with both hands from behind. My knees dig into the small of his back and I pull, with every little last ounce of strength I have left, I pull. He flaps under me, his right hand swollen to twice its original size, but he can't get out from under me. I continue, pulling, tearing. My teeth grind hard against each other and with one last strong tug, his cervical vertebrae snaps in several places, as I force down his lumbar vertebrae. He goes limp and I release him. I fall back, sucking in air and then I quickly choke, coughing blood on him. I push him with both hands and I'm once again standing, panting, and staring back toward the hospital from this side of the courtyard.

With a heavy sigh, the buzzer rings again loudly. I draw each breath closer and closer together, trying to focus my vision on the doors from my one functional eye. From them, walks a single woman. I don't know her now, but I'll meet her later; she is that nurse. She walks out into the cold, almost motionless, and completely naked. Her hair is vibrant cobalt yellow; it tosses about in the cold wind covering her face and then exposing it as she continues toward me. Her expression, like everyone else that has walked out, empty, but her emptiness is different. As though she doesn't know where she is or what she is doing here, and she definitely isn't charging at me like she is going to try—yes, try—to kill me. Let alone she doesn't notice she's naked and walking past several bodies. She just continues on. Her hips hypnotically sway with every step and with every step, she grows closer and closer to me. I can now make out every curve, every detail of her symmetrically fantastic frame. She comes to a dead stop in front of me, and stares at me.

"Kill her, Grey."

I stumble up to her and I slide my hands over her neck, I can feel the lace of her skin with my thumbs as they take their place behind her ears. She flinches. I cock her head back so I can see her eyes under her lengthy aureate bangs. Those empty cerulean pools, lost in their lids. I can see the change in expression, even how incremental it is; I see it in the side of her lips as I tighten my grip. I begin to whimper as I try and force my hands across her milky throat. She doesn't fight, but she moves her hands on my chest. I close the only eye I can and try harder to squeeze but I can't, my grip instead loosens as her hands are over my heart inside my gown, resting. I open my eye, and I see her diminutive change of expression, again at the corners of her lips and I can see the struggle to make that expression. I release her neck and step back.

"Grey. Kill her."

I undo my gown and remove it, throwing it over her. I stand in front of her, naked now, tying the gown up, and her hands go back to my chest. I smile.

From over her shoulder, I see Sketch. He walks toward us; I step around her and stand in front of her. Sketch subtly removes something from his jacket. I take a step forward and that is when I feel the barbs penetrate my flesh, instantaneously followed by incapacitating current, and I topple. I convulse on the ground, grabbing the tendrils attached to the barbs that are attached to what Sketch is holding. Sketch holds some sort of conductive energy device, which I can only guess is a taser, but I can't hold a thought because of the extremely powerful current pulsing through me. He walks up beside her and looks down at me,

"She's pretty, isn't she? Don't worry Grey; we will get you past this."

He runs his hand up the inside of her leg under the gown. She passively grunts as he pushes his fingers inside her. I try and stand,

"Whoa, Grey, relax."

I get to one knee, but I'm forced back to the

ground as he just holds that trigger down, and more and more current finds place through and through me.

She doesn't fight him, but I can see it in her face; her eyes are on me and as he pulls her head back and licks across her cheek, she cringes.

"Mmm, tasty."

From under her gown, his hand moves quicker and harder. She is limp in his arms, staring down at me. Again, I try and stand. He pulls his mouth from her neck and frowns,

"Have a little fun, Grey. Don't be so serious; it is bad for your health."

"Sketch sto…"

He presses the button again and the current tears at me, but this time I don't leave my knee, I don't fall back convulsing; I fight every single bit of the current that fights to overwhelm my muscles and the pain is so intense I feel like I'm going to black out, but I stay there. Every time he releases the button, I go to stand and this time he lets me, so immediately I try and charge him, but as soon as I move forward, I feel the current and careen to the side, losing all strength in every bit of my limps. I crash face first into the ground, flip on to my back, and gyrate violently next to him.

As I lose consciousness, I see a tear roll down her cheek, and I can tell she is disappointed in me.

"I'm sorry."

One single apology whispers out from my closed lips and clenched teeth, and then I black out.

When I open my eyes, I feel very disconnected. I've been unconscious and it feels like I've been that way for a very, very extended period of time. I only know this because my face doesn't hurt, and I can see out of both my eyes. I'm empty, void of what emotions I felt before I lost consciousness. I'm not angry with Sketch. I don't feel remorse for those I dispatched. I don't have any guilt about not helping the nurse. I'm actually happy about snapping Deshane's neck. However, I am confused as to how I'm repaired, I don't remember recovering and I don't know how long I have been unconscious. I'm also staring at a pattern on the acoustic ceiling planks; each plank has tiny punctures, the kind of punctures that look like a pencil had impaled and fell from, but that is just how they are made. The kind they have in schools and older offices. I look down and around. I'm sitting up in a metal chair in front of a metal table in the middle of a room. Pale white walls that have been repainted time and time again surround me. One door across from me with a small plate glass window and from behind the door, I hear a conversation happening. Only whispers, so I can't make out what they are saying.

I look at my hands. Small healing cuts on them imply I've been unconscious for a week, maybe two.

Some cuts deeper than others, and some more regenerated than others.

My thoughts are interrupted by the sound of a mechanical beep, indicating the door is about to open. I sit back, placing my hands in my lap. I keep my eyes fixed and waiting for whoever is walking in; they have my attention.

From the door walks a man. This is the first time—well, the first time I remember—meeting him. His name is Silk Crisante. He looks about my age, even though I don't know how old I am. He has my build. My height: he has my hair color, even my eye color; deep brown, almost cherry.

"Hey Greyor, how do you feel?"

"Disconnected. I feel like I have been asleep for a week. What happened?"

"What do you remember?"

"The courtyard."

"Good."

"Good?"

"You have to remember that place. It'll help."

"Help with what?"

"It will help you get better. It will help you remember."

"Who are you?"

"Sorry Grey. I thought you might remember me."

He cracks a smile, leaning his head down, catching

my gaze.

"No, I don't. Sorry."

"People usually remember me. No worries, Grey. You will next time. I'm Silk. Silk Crisante. It is a pleasure, again."

He smiles a very familiar smile, like we're good friends, like I've known him my whole life.

"Pleasure is all yours."

I say expressionlessly, staring coldly at him from under my brow.

"Ouch. Greyor. Really?"

"Really."

"Oh, well. Listen, Grey, you have to do what Sketch says. You can't let those people get to you. It is you or them. They're gone..."

He taps on his temple.

"Nothing is coming back for them. They're mindless. I mean, they were like us, and Alrick's pills tried to give them a second chance, but they didn't benefit like we did. Those people aren't ever going to be people again..."

I interject.

"That is because I killed them."

"No, Greyor, consciously they were already dead. I mean, they were like animals, sick animals. You put them down. If the medication doesn't work, it cleans house."

"What do you mean 'cleans house'?"

"I mean, those people did things we did and got caught. Instead of just rotting away, they were given a second chance, like us. The only thing is the medication trials didn't help them change, it failed them, but it is helping us."

"Helping us what?"

"Become someone else."

"I don't even know who I am. Why would I want to become someone else?"

"Because who you were did a lot of damage, hurt a lot of people that didn't deserve getting hurt. Greyor, you have a second chance to be a part of society."

"I may not remember anything, but I do know killing people is wrong."

"You know that now because you're recovering. But those people from the courtyard weren't people. They stopped being people the moment they took innocent lives; the moment they destroyed someone else's life. Sadly, they don't get a second chance; the pills didn't work, but they're working on us. Helping us recognize the difference between thought and action, between right and wrong. Do you understand, Greyor?"

"No."

"You will man, you have to trust me on this."

"I doubt I will, and I don't have to trust you."

"You will. You have to trust your friends. You have to remember that courtyard because you will be back in it soon enough. Cleaning up the people who don't deserve a second chance and that courtyard is going to help you function out there. It will help you with the work you'll be doing soon. We have to ensure the only people who get a second chance, deserve it."

I sigh, sitting up and adjusting my posture. He goes into his pockets and removes a Zippo and a pack of cigarettes. He removes a brown tipped cigarette, tossing it into his lips with uncanny accuracy. It lands between his teeth that now shine, smiling. He lights the end and takes a deep breath, adjusting his own posture, getting comfortable, and he stares at me.

"Sorry Grey, did you want one?"

"I don't smoke."

"You sure about that?"

He is right. I'm not sure. It smells phenomenal and I'm drawn to it, like I know it, like I've missed it, but I just shake my head, declining.

"Alright. So, Greyor, what do you remember?"

Before speaking I catch myself, I'm about to admit in words that I remember something. I suddenly trust him. I stop myself.

"Nothing."

"I asked you a pretty general question. You can't say anything. You must remember something. I mean, you remember the courtyard, right?"

He smiles.

"I remember the courtyard."

I smile.

"Greyor."

He says disappointingly.

"I remember things. I can't place them. I can't throw them into properly formed sentences because I only remember clips. Moments. Not names, places, or time. I remember caring about someone. Caring to the point where their emotional state would change my emotional state. Like I was a part of them, and they were a part of me. I remember losing someone. That someone...that someone I shared that connection with. I can't remember who they are. I can't remember who I was or when I lost them, but I still feel that emptiness. Right now."

He takes a deep breath, sucking down a large drag of the cigarette before blowing one ring of smoke and then another, followed by a third. He sits up, letting the remainder of the smoke rush from his nose. He squints and then smiles.

"I know how that is, man. I was the same at first. It will pass. That is the feeling of losing yourself, your old self, slowly dissipating. I promise man, that will pass, and it will get easier to build new memories. But you have to let go of that. You have to forget that to move on. We're a lot more alike than you think. I mean, hell, that is why they let me talk to you. They think it'll help you and to be honest, I think it will too."

"I don't need any help, Silk."

His expression changes behind the smoke screen. He leans forward whispering.

"Alright Greyor, listen, I don't like Sketch either. You can't escape this man. You must accept it or we're not getting out of here. I know where you are right now and trust me, it doesn't get any better. Play along. You get to leave once and awhile. Or they will keep shocking you, and medicating you, and keep throwing you in that courtyard until it sinks in. This is your life now. The sooner you accept that, the sooner it will make sense. Do what they tell you and you get to live man. You want to live, right?"

I lean forward.

"Why didn't you just start with that? And why are you telling me this? They have to be listening. If you say you've been where I am, how does this not bother you? That you can't remember who you are? That you are tortured daily to forget one thing and forced to remember something else? I mean, Silk, if we're good buddies like you say we are, then how are you ok with this?"

He leans in even closer.

"Greyor, that is too many questions for me to

answer without them interrupting. Do me a favor. Play along." He leans back, blowing smoke, retaking the comfortable lean he had before he came in to talk to me.

"You're a lot smarter than you look, do you know that, Greyor?"

"So do you Silk, so do you."

He smiles. I smile. He smokes. I watch him smoke.

CHRISTINA PERKINS

Name sound familiar? It should, I killed her boyfriend, Christopher Helm. The first policy I had the pleasure of executing for Grim Associations; my job, my life, and the only consistent factor in my so-called life. Do I fill her policy? No, I don't kill her, but I get to watch someone else do it. This is how I get to know Silk Crisante. Silk, my only friend, or the only thing I have that gets even close to resembling one. This is the first time I get to see his work.

We're at a club called Chaos. I'm not sure if Silk knows I'm here, but I know he is somewhere lost in the mob of people crowding the floor and packed in tables. I know Christina is here, too, somewhere lost in the masses. I come through the coat check. A young vibrant woman smiles at me, beckons for me to check my coat, but I smile politely and walk on because if I check my coat my M1911A1 would be in plain sight, and I don't think security would let me stay. I excuse my way through one mob of women and men mingling, yelling over the music to try and learn about one another. Pressed and packed tightly together while music drowns out the conversation right next to them. They couldn't hear what the next couple is saying even if they were trying to. I continue on, smiling and excusing myself at every push and bump of someone I pass by. Some women stop me with a smile, hold me back to talk to them, and so every time, I politely motion them to wait, and I'll be right back. I do this all with a simple lip sink and index finger gesture, feigning the motion of "I'll be back in a second".

However, I don't come back. I just move on and on through the crowd.

In a booth, I see Christina. She's with a couple of girlfriends, chatting away. I look over and there is Silk, standing off to the side, sipping a drink, standing alone, but appearing to be part of a dancing group of men and women. He soaks up the atmosphere comfortably. Unhinged, or so it appears, by the group prancing around him. He is still and motionless while people spin, waddle, shutter, and shake around him. He would stand out if someone was sober enough to pay attention. He is paying attention. His focus is Christina. I get closer and I wonder if he knows I'm here. More so, does he know Sketch is here, outside, looking for him. Furthermore, does Sketch know I'm here?

I move around and behind group after group of strangers, and at every couple of steps, someone stops me. First, it is a girl who grinds into me. Her ass finds home in my crotch as she shakes and gyrates to the music, looking back at me, smiling madly. I get a wink and move off her. Second, a man that looks at me, smiling and taking a step back. He thinks he knows me; he screams something—not a word, more like a grunt—and then asks as loudly as he can,

"What's up, bro?"

I smile, extending it to a huge fake smile, nodding my head to his rhythm, signing the words,

"What?"

As though I'm confirming he knows me and that this is what is actually up; this club, it is what's up, it is wild.

As soon as he can't see my expression, it changes violently, as I shake it off with a sigh.

The third person to stop me is a person bumping into me and then holding me back to apologize. I recognize the accident immediately without thought and try to persist on. She stops me dead in my tracks and apologizes again. I smile and nod and let her know I understand it was an accident and I'm going to move on, except she doesn't let me. No, she makes another apology. She really needs the confirmation that I really know it was an accident, like there will be consequences if I don't accept her apology or, more so, if she doesn't get that apology across. I stop. I look deeply into her eyes. I keep her attention. I smile and I lip the words,

"It's ok."

She smiles, lips the word,

"Ok."

And she disappears back into the crowd that she came from.

I get through the crowd, and I've lost sight of Silk. I turn my direction to Christina, and she is still chatting away. She's in a crescent shaped booth, packed tightly and neatly amongst other under-dressed and over-made-up women. They smile concurrently, laugh simultaneously, and concentrate on only one another. Simple conversations lead to laughter rising and falling. They all seem to be more focused on Christina, as though they're celebrating her, or consoling her.

I wonder if they know that she was Christopher's mistress. That the money from his death is paying for some, if not all, of those drinks and that money should have been left to Loraine Helm, Christopher's wife.

That is an odd thing to wonder?

In my wonder, I don't notice Silk walk right up to Christina's table and completely end their conversation with a sentence; a sentence that the group of girls at Christina's table responds with a synchronous, thought interrupting, completely captivating, awe.

I crack my neck in how fast I try to turn to look at the table, try to comprehend what happened. I'm shocked because the entire table's focus is on Silk, they are hypnotized by him. I can see him talk, I can't see his lips, but his gesture; he talks with his body. His arms, shoulders, and torso move with his speech. They don't stop smiling and awing. Glancing at each other, completely confirming the same thing; they all think he is sweet. Silk looks back, beyond me, and beyond the dance floor mob of people to the DJ, who he nods too. As he looks back the music changes. A song by Kissing with Pop Rocks comes on; I think it's called Names of Cities. He extends his hand, and the girls begin to rise, moving out of Christina's way. They head toward the floor, and I move back into the crowd.

Wonder what he said?

I'm not supposed to be here. I have a policy to fill.

Why are you here then?

Silk isn't supposed to be here. He has a policy to fill.

Why do you care what Silk is doing?

I don't know. Curiosity, maybe, maybe he can be an ally.

Are you mental?

Yes, that is already as evident as it can be.

I step back, deeper into the crowd, walking slowly backward almost sideways. The music is slower. Couples are dancing and singles move off the floor. Before the group is completely broken, I grab a girl by the arm and pull her into me. I look down and smile. Surprised and stumbled she smiles at me and then rests her head on my chest and we slowly circle the floor.

Feels like an elementary school dance, and now, yep, now we're dancing.

I draw her in and I lead us just outside the group of dancing couples. Trying to get closer and closer to Silk, I want to hear what they're talking about. When I get in ear shot, this is the first thing I hear,

"This is why I come out...On a rare occasion you really get to appreciate someone beautiful."

Christina responds, her response so close, it sounds like she almost cut him off.

"You're just saying that. Saying I'm beautiful."

"No...no...I'm not. I mean it. You're so beautiful. So...endearing...to the point that I've completely ditched my friends to just get your name, sure, I took it a step further. I get a dance and to be introduced to you and all your pretty friends."

"They're just pretty?"

"Yeah, you're beautiful. They're pretty."

Silk smirks and shoots off a little wink and despite the darkness and dancing light, I can tell, she is blushing.

My head is wrenched down, and my lips are overwhelmed by my partners. She has thrown my balance and stopped our dance as she eats my face. She pulls away as she jostles my hair,

"Oh my god...you're so hot. I mean, like, really hot. Has anyone ever told you that?"

I smile, looking back over at Silk and Christina.

"Is that your ex-girlfriend or something?"

I look back at my dance partner shaking my head no, almost giggling. She grabs me and kisses me again. I kiss back for a few seconds before tearing free and looking back over.

"Oh! I just noticed that. He is like...your twin brother?"

What?

I look back at her, my expression wracked by confusion. I shake my head and look back over, but Silk and Christina aren't there. I look around but before I get a full view of the club, my partner grabs me and tries to kiss me. She pulls away making a show of it and then she runs her hands up my chest and stops right before my neck.

"Oh my god, ask already."

"Ask what?"

"To take me home."

"Why would I do that?"

Come on.

"Oh my god, you're so funny, but seriously, are we going to go?"

If she mentions God one more time, I swear...

"Wait here, I just need to use the washroom, and I'll come get you so we can leave."

Out into the crowd I'm gone. I head toward the

washroom. I make it look like I'm about to go down, I get down two stairs before sliding back up the stair well on the opposite wall and I come out of view of the dance floor and make it out the front door on to the bustling night street. I walk out past the door men, past the long patient line, past the crowd of smokers and I see Silk and Christina walking down a side street. I stand behind part of the smoker's crowd shielding myself from Sketch's view. He is sitting in a parked car on the other side of the crowd. I tap the closest person to me on the shoulder,

"Hey, isn't that...oh shit it is, look who it is."

They immediately look over, identifying who I was pointing at, and make some guess who they think it is, but I don't catch what the person says because Sketch is now looking at what that guy and the rest of the smokers think they see in their inebriation.

I take off after them walking quickly but not quick enough to draw attention to myself. I stop at where the streets meet and peer around. Silk is climbing into the passenger seat of Christina's car, laughing.

"Your place it is."

He shuts the door and the car starts.

I turn around and head back to my car. I quickly come to the driver's side door when a voice startles me. I turn and there in front of me is my dance partner.

"Oh, that's how it is?"

"What?"

Without a response she comes at me, her foot flying toward my scrotum with testicle crushing speed. She intends to make my testicles retreat into my gut. I catch her leg swinging and hold it in my hand, smiling,

"Nice legs."

She pulls her foot back as I limply let it go.

"Listen, I'm sorry, but remember my brother? Well, he just left, and he wanted me to check my car for his keys just in case he needs to go home, which, I don't think he has to worry about because..."

"Wow, ok, I'm like so sorry. I just assumed you were ditching and I..."

She smiles at me, cocking her head to the side and deeply exhales,

"...thought we had something."

"Totally, same here, I wasn't leaving...come on...I mean, you, me, the dance floor? It was..."

"Yeah, I know, right? It was...I mean...wow...it was hot. So, you wanna go?"

"Yeah...about that...I really have to get these keys to my brother."

"Will you call me after?"

"Of course."

I open the door and get in but before I can close it, she steps between the door and the car.

"Um. Forgetting something?"

"What?"

Her number hot stuff.

"My phone number! Oh my god...you are so...cute."

"Yeah. Wow. Sorry. What is it?"

"555-9090"

I open my phone; I throw her number in it, and quickly close it. I try to close my door, but she doesn't move, she only sighs, and rolls her eyes.

"What?"

"Don't you want to know my name?"

"Ha. Yeah, my, I don't know where my head is at. Sorry. What is your name beautiful?"

She smiles, slides her hand on my face, and pulls my chin up and kisses me softly.

"My name is Elaine, sweetie."

"Well Elaine, the pleasure is all mine, it was very nice meeting you, but I really have to go. I'll call you later."

She moves closer.

"Not so fast. I want to know who is calling me and you need to text me your number right now. I have a face, I want a number, and a name."

"My number is 612-7617."

She takes her time inputting it, looking from the phone to me and from me to the phone before looking back up and staring at me with a blank look.

"My name is Johnny."

There it is again.

"Nice to meet you, Johnny."

She smiles, coming in for a kiss. I quickly kiss her lips and pull away smiling adjusting myself to the driver seat. She backs up and I close the door and start the car, quickly taking off, leaving her standing in the parking lot watching me leave.

As I drive, I navigate the internet on my phone looking up Christina's Street. I know her address and I know her phone number. I already know a lot about Christina because of Christopher and yes, though I'm not supposed to, we both know, I remember the details. I just don't know how to get to her house.

I get my route, dodging main streets, cutting down through the best parts of suburban living. I arrive at her house forty-five minutes later. I see her car parked in the driveway. I drive past her house and park several houses down, half-way between the third and fourth house past hers.

I sit back in my seat turning the ignition off. I wait. I wait ten minutes before looking back and checking for signs of life. No traffic through this street. Nobody walks by. Nobody is outside or anywhere in sight. I get out of my car, I walk down toward her house, and I stop right before her house's lawn, and I wait. I don't see movement. All the lights are off. The front porch has a small three step stoop bordered by a black cast iron rail. Leading up to the stoop is a small concrete walkway, dividing her front lawn into two sections. The driveway touches the right side. The left side leads around the house to the backyard. Overgrown lilac bushes cover the path, but it is there.

What're you doing here?

I want to know what he is going to do.

Why do you care?

I'm curious.

I see the light come on over the front stoop. Motion activated maybe; I can't tell from where I'm standing. I'm blind, standing dead center of the left side part of the lawn, switching my attention from the front door and the path off to the side. I hear a click, a turn of a lock popping open. I'm off the lawn and back on the sidewalk walking back toward my car. I hear the front door open coupled by the sound of my soles on the concrete. I quicken my pace toward the car. I hear voices quickly followed by the door shutting and followed directly by footsteps and whistling. I'm at my car door when I hear a voice.

"Greyor?"

I stop and slowly look over.

"What're you doing here buddy?"

"What're you doing here?"

Silk's expression stunned his face wrinkles, and he raises his eyebrows.

"Greyor, come on, I assumed we were past this?"

He walks over to the passenger side door and stops removing a pack of cigarettes. He opens the pack, pulls out two, throws one in his mouth and rolls the other at me over the roof of the car. I hear a chime as he opens a Zippo flicking at the wheel drawing a heavy flame tearing at the wick. He brings the inferno up to his face as he smiles, drawing in a large breath. He looks at me. He looks at the cigarette that rolls and stops in front of my hand.

"Grey, I've learned—not so recently either—but I've learned that I need things. One of those things is a girl like Christina, momentarily of course and this..."

He lifts his cigarette flicking ash off the end on to the roof of the car.

"Yet another momentary fixation but I am..."

He smiles.

"Fixed."

I stare blankly at him.

"What... was she a policy?"

He shakes his head blowing smoke from his nostrils widening his smile. His expression immediately changes as he looks at me again.

"No. Greyor. She is a person. They're all people. How much of that shit do they have you on?"

I shrug. As I feel my hand look and find the bottle of pills in my coat pocket.

"Guess what Greyor. I don't take that shit. The medication."

I stay silent.

"They have you on that because you can't do what I can do."

"What would that be?"

"Fill these "policies". Go back to Southstone willingly, get some sleep, and then go take another life. Your mind can't handle it. Not many people could. Those people in the courtyard are like you..."

I cut him off.

"I thought you said..."

"I know what I said. No one is listening now. So, I'm telling you the truth, the whole of it. You don't have to take that medication to play along. You can do it willingly. Get your work done and go home. Just prove yourself and leniency will be yours..."

"So, what exactly from last time we spoke was true?"

"Oh, you remember our conversation. That is odd. Because you shouldn't, that was weeks ago, but here you are making memories."

I go stiff. He knows I remember. His voice changes my unease.

"Greyor. Relax. I'm not your enemy. I've seen it in

your eyes. You play the part, but I can tell even if they can't. You're starting to remember and don't worry, that is our secret."

"Silk. Do you know who I am?"

"No. But I can help you find out. The question is do you want to know?"

"Yes."

"Alright, Greyor. Don't you have a "policy" to fill?"

"Yeah. I do."

I roll the smoke back to him as he throws his away. He picks it up and slides it behind his ear. He looks at the door and then looks back at me.

"Well, you better go do that. Can I get a ride?"

"Yeah. Get in."

I jump in, unlock the passenger side door and start the car. I start to drive.

"So why did you follow me here?"

"I know Christina doesn't have an expired policy."

"You mean we're not supposed to kill her? Actually, she does have a policy with us. It is part of the original insurance clause with Christopher, who I'm sure you remember?"

"Yeah, I remember Christopher. Are you going to kill Christina?"

"She's already dead."

"But I heard you talking to her?"

"She'll be dead soon."

"How?"

"Awe Greyor, the things you don't know…"

He removes the smoke from behind his ear, lights the cigarette, draws a breath, and looks at me.

"It may come to you as a surprise, but I'm special, and not in a mentally handicapped way either…"

I cut him off.

"Then how? What makes you special?"

"Chemistry."

"Chemistry?"

"As it turns out I have a very, very, very rare disorder. That is why Grim Associations recruited me."

"Well, what is it?"

Silk laughs.

"I'm poisonous."

I stop looking at the road and stare over at him, I look for the comedy, I try and find the joke. He sits back smoking and smiling.

"You're poisonous?"

"Isn't that what I just said?"

"Care to elaborate?"

"It is pretty self-explanatory, but, for your sake, why not. I secrete poison, it is in my blood, in my salvia, in my…"

He makes a jerking motion with his fist.

"I get it. Thanks for that visual. I don't understand though, first, how do you know? And second, how does it—and I'm only assuming here —but how does it kill?"

He stops giggling and takes a large drag of his smoke.

"Her name was Michelle. First girl I ever had sex with. I was crazy about her... absolutely nuts about her, she was the only one I ever wanted to spend time with..."

"How old were you?"

"Sixteen...So, we fuck, day later, she's dead. I was destroyed. Down and out. I didn't understand what happened. Then it happened again and again and again. The always died from the same thing..."

"What actually killed them?"

"Too much dopamine, somehow, I secrete it. Don't get me wrong of all the ways to go being in a constant state of euphoria ain't that bad..."

"They were over stimulated. And you somehow think you're responsible?"

"I am, tried, tested, and true. I'm fucking Michelin."

"What?"

"Like the tires...never mind. The all died the same way, too much dopamine. Their bodies overheat and the major organs shut down. They all look like drug overdose victims. The coroners could never identify what drug caused the overdose. I'm that drug."

"That isn't possible."

"Oh, it isn't? That is funny coming from you."

"What is that supposed to mean?"

"You'll know soon enough. Anyways, if you don't believe me, go check on Christina tomorrow."

"Ok, hypothetically speaking, if you are poisonous, why kill Christina?"

"Because she made me her beneficiary..."

Silk looks out the window, letting his sentence trail off, almost covering the last part up by mumbling.

I laugh. He looks over at me, unimpressed.

"Why the fuck would she do that?"

"I told her too."

"Because you told her to? And that's it? And boom...she, does it?"

"Because she loves me..."

I burst out laughing, almost driving us into a parked car. I look over at him and he appears extremely intrigued by something.

"Didn't you just meet her tonight?"

"Yep. Do you realize you have been laughing and continuing to laugh?"

I stop laughing, breathing, and functioning momentarily. Then I gain composure as I divide my attention between Silk and the road. He is right. I'm laughing. I don't remember laughing. I haven't laughed in...

"Hey!" I look over at Silk who starts giggling again.

"How the hell is she in love with you?"

He smiles, lights yet another smoke, and just stares at me.

"Silk?"

"I'm poison Grey. The same thing I secrete that kills them is the same thing that makes them think they're in love with me."

Silk sits back blowing a plume of smoking across the roof of the car that glides and hangs over us, he grows silent, staring up at the smoke.

"Silk, I'm..."

"Come on Grey."

My grip tightens around the wheel. I look from him to the road, taking another corner, driving on and on with no destination. I know I'm not going anywhere but I'm not sure if he does.

"So, this is why you work for Grim Associations? Doing what we do?"

"What else am I supposed to do? The life I had I left behind and for good reason. I can't live what most would call a normal life. Grim Associations at least gave me a purpose. Someone loses but at least it's painless..."

"Are you sure about that?"

"I feel a lot better Grey, thanks, you really know how to cheer a friend up."

I look at him and now he's at least smiling. I recognize its fake; I know he isn't happy; how could he be? How could anyone be? Doing what we do or being who we are. I may not have memories, but these aren't memories I want. Poor Silk doesn't have that choice. Every time he gets close to someone, if he touches them, kisses them, loves them, they die. I may not fully comprehend misery, but that is a miserable existence.

Poor bastard.

"Silk?"

He sits up.

"Yeah Greyor?"

"What did you mean when you said: That's funny coming from you?"

"You can't die."

"What do you mean I can't die?"

"I might withdraw the remark about you being smart Grey, I'm considering it."

"I mean it Silk; what do you mean I can't die?"

"Let me rephrase then. You're terrible at dying. They have tried, time and time again, but you just won't die."

I look at him in disbelief, but he nods pompously at me.

"So, when you say they?"

"I mean Grim Associations. They have put you

through so much, pushed and pushed. They shot you, stabbed you, shocked you, time and time again you survive the courtyard. You name it, they have tried it, but your heart keeps on beating. I thought I was special but you Grey, you're a fucking machine..."

His sentence cut short by his phone ringing. He pulls it from his pocket and stares at it, stares at it as though he is afraid to answer.

"Silk? Who is it?"

"It's..."

He clears his throat to find his voice as it almost cut out.

"Christina."

"Are you going to answer it?"

He looks down at the phone, his face sours, his lids squint and his lips quiver. He is completely bereaved, absent from everything and anything he had moments ago. His smile is long gone and with a single tear the phone stops ringing as it goes to voice mail. He shakes to remove a cigarette from his pack, forcing the brown tip in and past his lips and he bites down on the filter. Subtly, my hand goes to the car's cigarette lighter. I push it in. It takes him several moments to find his lighter even though it's sitting on the dash, but he can't light his smoke. He tries and tries, and more sparks illuminate the dark interior of the car, finally, and he snaps throwing the lighter against the dashboard. At the moment it strikes, the cigarette lighter pops out, announcing it is ready for use. I grab it and light his cigarette. He draws in what seems like an endless breath before looking over at me, nodding in thanks. I nod back.

He looks at his phone.

"I'm going to the play the message."

I look over at him, eyebrows slightly raised, questioning his choice with expression alone.

"I know. I know. I shouldn't. But I want too."

He unlocks his phone and dials his voicemail. He presses one button to bring the message from playing through the earpiece to playing through the speaker. So, we can hear it, even though I never said I wanted to.

The message fills the silence of the car,

"I still can't stop shaking...wow...Silk...that was amazing. Hey...its...well you know who it is...I just wanted to say...I mean...I had such a wonderful night...Silk...I've never met someone like...I mean no one has ever made me feel this way...not even Christopher..."

Silk closes his eyes as she pauses.

"...I want to see you again Silk. I want to see you again soon...I hope...no...I know you feel...I know you feel the same because...because you can't fake the way you look at me...or how you touch me...Silk, I really wish you would've stayed…It would've been…It would've been…it would've been so…"

No more words, just a thud, gurgling, and moaning which continues for about thirty seconds and then a wheeze followed by choking noises and then silence. The message continues until Silks voicemail cuts it off.

My eyes wander to the clock and I'm not far from where I should be right now. Remember earlier when I said I had no destination, well actually I do, I was killing time. I had a policy to fill. That policy is Timothy Busch. He will be leaving work in five minutes and I'm a block away. My foot subtly presses down on the accelerator. I pick up speed. Silk, despite his state, notices and even with the water welling in his eyes he looks at me.

"Grey?"

The light up ahead goes yellow, I press the accelerator to the floor. I see Timothy at the crosswalk as he goes to walk, I turn off my headlights.

"Greyor?"

The speedometer climbs and climbs while the rpm red lines. I flick on the headlights, but it is already too late for Timothy. When he hits the windshield, it shatters but it doesn't break, his body dents the hood, and I slam on the breaks. The rubber peels to the asphalt leaving a path behind the car. He flies off and careens down the empty road. With the sleeves of my coat, I wipe off the steering wheel and open my door with it. I step out and Silk is stunned.

"Time to go."

"What the fuck?"

I walk off this street and down another street connecting to it. I look back to see Silk heading the opposite direction. I get around the corner and I hear people shouting, running, identifying that somebody was just hit; yelling for someone to call an ambulance but Timothy is dead, because he died on impact. As I corner another street my phone rings, it is Elaine.

"Hello?"

"You said you would call."

"I was just about to."

"Can I see you? Are you busy?"

"Nope. I'll come by, where do you live?"

TROUBLE AT SOUTHSTONE

Silk was right. Christina died from a dopamine overdose. Her body shut down; organs failed, she overheated and died. Silk listened to her die. What a miserable way to live, I wonder how he's doing.

Why do you care?

He's, my friend.

Last time you saw him, he was crying, and you ran somebody over.

I'm submerged in a tub; water almost escapes its mass. With my nose I breach the glassy surface, and with my eyes open, I watch each bubble drift to the surface. I can hear the muffled sounds outside the water; I can hear a clock somewhere ticking away. I'm unsure how long it has been. I don't know when I last left Southstone or how they picked me up. I was retrieved but don't remember it happening. The medication is starting to cloud my memories. I've noticed that my dosage has increased incredibly since the last time I checked the daily milligram dose, and I don't remember the last time I checked it. You take pills long enough, you lose count of when you take them, or how many you have taken that day. When the side effects hit, you begin to forget what day it is- if you remembered what day it was in the first place. For me, time sometimes feels like mesh or chain links, it is stuck together with each link connected to the next without a break in between.

I told you not to take them.

From outside the tub, I hear something chiming, over and over the sound repeats. My head breaks the surface of the water, and I look around. As the water runs from my ears, I can hear what sounds like an alarm; annoyingly beeping, over, and over, and over. I also notice I'm no longer alone. Standing near the entrance of the shower room is that nurse, the blonde one. She's pressed up against the doorway and almost appears as if she's hiding. She is stunned as she realizes she is also not alone. She looks afraid – wait, she is showing signs of emotion, of consciousness – and now I'm standing up in the tub.

"I'm not going to hurt you."

"Where the fuck am I?"

"You don't remember me, do you?"

"I said, where the fuck am I?"

She is now screaming. As she finishes her sentence she pulls a gun.

"Where did you get that?"

"Are you deaf?"

"No, but I'm not your enemy, now relax."

"Where the fuck am I?"

"It wouldn't matter if I told you. If you don't remember me, you won't remember where you are."

"Do I know you?"

"I was told to kill you..."

I step out of the tub. She lifts the gun.

You're naked. I wouldn't move, man. She isn't fucking around. She is terrified. Why the hell would you even mention that?

"I defended you and I got shocked and tortured for it. I'm not your enemy. Now, what is your name?"

"My name?"

"Yes, your name. What can I call you?"

"My name is Riley."

"Riley, I'm Greyor."

"What kind of fucking name is Greyor?"

She screams at me, shaking the gun.

"Riley, please, please put down the gun."

"No. I want to go home."

"Do you know where home is?"

She looks around. She then shakes her head vigorously. Tears well up, and then they start pouring.

"Please. Please. Please...don't hurt me."

She buckles, falling on the floor, pulling her knees to her chest.

"I'm not going to hurt you. I'm going to approach you and I'm sorry I'm naked, but I was bathing, and you busted in here. Is that ok?"

She just begins sobbing. I walk over and when I get there I go to my knees. I put my hands on her face, pulling her to look at me.

"We don't have much time. What do you remember?"

"My name is Riley..." She pauses. "I was working...tables...at...I was waiting..."

She sobs louder and louder, losing her ability to speak. I hear footsteps. Several people running in our direction from outside the shower room, outside in the hall, they're coming for her.

"Listen you have to trust me. We're out of time. Do you trust me?"

She looks up. Her eyes are puffy, and snot is running out of her nose. She nods pathetically, sucking in air as she attempts to form a sentence. I lift her up and as I walk toward the bath, I kick the gun she was holding under a locker. I look down at her.

"Hold your breath."

I sink back into the large pool with her, water spills over; she sucks in air as I push her under water. The soap has diluted the once transparent water, making it opaque so she disappears under the surface. Just as I sink to my chest, Sketch, the twins, and two others run into the room.

"Greyor!"

"Yeah?"

They all look around. The twins walk past Sketch, checking the change rooms, looking in lockers, under benches, looking in every hiding spot. Sketch takes a couple steps forward,

"Has anyone come in here?"

He looks around, loudly chewing a piece of gum.

"Nope."

"You haven't seen a blonde girl?"

I feign confusion.

"No?"

I feel her hands on my stomach, clawing, she's running out of air. I force her head and body down subtly.

"Sure, about that?"

"I would have noticed a blonde girl."

"Hurry the fuck up and get back to your quarters. We're locking this place down. If you see a blonde girl, grab the bitch and hold her for me, ok?"

"Will do."

He motions for the twins to follow him and the others out. They both synchronously look at me and then look away at the same moment.

She stopped moving.

She wasn't under that long.

When they leave and I can't hear their voices I quickly tear her from the water. She's motionless. I shake her and within a second she takes a huge inhale, coughing on me. She takes several large breaths in, staring at me. Her eyes again wince, and she begins to cry.

"It's ok. You're ok."

I bring her to my chest.

Through the coughing and crying I make out something she says.

"Please get me out of here. I want to go home."

I hold her in my arms. Compared to me, she is small and appears fragile. She just cries and cries, nestling under my chin.

"Thank you Greyor."

I move her off of me gently. I climb out of the tub and grab my grey sweatpants. I look out into the hallway for signs of motion but no one is there. I feel hands on my back. I turn and she's shivering behind me. I grab a nearby towel and wrap her in it.

"Come on. You have to be quiet. Ok?"

She nods. I take her hand and begin running down the hallway. I stop at the corner where two halls meet; I listen. When I don't hear anything, I pull her, running again. We run by the living quarters' hallway, and I slide to a stop as I notice that every door is open. Every single door of the hallway is open. I look at her,

"Did you do this?"

She cringes her face and nods.

"How?"

"I woke up in front of this man... I was in a room... it must have been some sort of a control room, it had small screens, a lot of screens, buttons and switches... and cables... that man was...he had me...I hit him, again and again...he was in a lab coat. When he was unconscious, I hit a bunch of buttons and switches trying to get out of the room. I must have opened these rooms when I..."

"Yeah, you must have, that means I can get you out of here, but I have to do something first."

She grabs my arm and tugs me.

"First? No. We have to get out of here now!"

She tugs but I don't turn. I stand motionless and stare at one place. A door at the end of the hallway, at the far end of the living quarters: a door that until this moment has always remained closed. I stiffen my muscles to tense and relax them, unhinging my unease. I turn and look at her, who still motions for us to leave. I look at her, relaxing my jaw intending to speak and then forcefully do,

"I will get you out of here. Ok? I promise. I won't let anything happen to you; but first, first, I need to know what's in that room...I point at the open door, the double door, the double reinforced mechanically locked, hermetically sealed double door.

The one room in this entire hallway without a plate glass window to look in, and the one room in this entire hallway that needs biometric identification to enter; that is always closed but now is open.

"... You can wait for me here, my room, or come with me, or you can leave right now. That is your choice. But I have to know what is in that room."

Her face changes: each crinkle around every freckle, her eyes squint and her mouth purses, she starts to weep uncontrollably. I pull her along, almost dragging her toward the room, her heels squeal on the floor. She sobs and I quietly and steadily press on. I get a step away from the doorway and she speaks.

"Please...please...let's go...let's leave...why do you need to know? What does it matter?"

I don't say anything as I walk in, dragging her behind.

This room is twice the size of my living quarters, and for good reason. Dead smack in the middle of it there is some sort of iron tank. Cables and wires snake out of several holes in the wall and they either connect to the tank or the computer terminal fixed next to it. The lighting in this room is miserable either intended to be very dim or the bulbs have almost all burned out. It is cold in here, colder than just several feet outside the room. A level of dust on the floor and footprints signifies this room is rarely opened. I look back to her and from behind her I notice a sign on the other side of the door it reads, "Do Not Disturb". My eyes don't stay on her. I look back at the iron tank, it sweats moisture. This tank is full, but of what?

I take a couple steps forward before she tugs me back.

"Please…let's go."

I hear footsteps echoing down the hallway, far away, maybe from the other side of the complex, from the halls adjacent to the living quarters or maybe a floor above. I don't look at her or acknowledge her. I walk to the large tank and investigate it. It is about ten feet long and eight feet wide. It is made from cast iron with steel riveted brackets and it is old, very old, at least half a century old. There are small monitors and smaller keyboards at the terminal. Information spews down and then I notice one specific monitor. It shows information, like the kind a heart monitor has, and that is when I hear the faint palpation. That of a blip but a change in the constant buzz from that specific monitor, that of a heartbeat, very weak but alive. Palpating. The closer I get, the stronger and faster the palpations become.

"Someone is inside that thing."

I walk around the tank, checking all of its sides. I make a full rotation before I notice the plaque looking thing engraved on its front. It reads,

Ian Hane —All humans are impulses away from beasts. Look closely and there it is, waiting. I looked and liked what I saw, so, I became the very thing we run from being. To the masses, one day, I will show myself.

0356

I instantly know that number. My hand tears into my sweatpants, pulling from them that little saffron bottle. I look at the label. If you have a medication bottle nearby, look at it, the label usually reads several things. You will have the RX number, which is specific to subscription or prescription, depending on if you get them from a drugstore. It may sometimes be a combination of numbers and letters. Across from that will be your name. Then there will be the doctor's name, usually. There will be number of tablets followed by the name of the drug and how many milligrams. Then there should be a DIN, which means drug identification number. Sometimes between the doctor's name and the drug name and how much you'll be taking is the literal name for what you're taking. My label probably doesn't look like yours but what is similar is the drug identification number, my bottle has one, and it is,

0356-7677

Next to the plaque is a small window with a cover. I hear in the distance, footsteps. She tugs on my arm, but I ignore her and open the window. I look inside the tank, and I see what lives inside. A man floats, strapped to some sort of apparatus, with tubes and wires running from him. The majority run from his head. Tubes are penetrating his skull and the wires run from leads strapped to his chest. He is directly connected to the computer terminal. Some of those tubes move from inside— from inside his skull—run off the tank to an outside pipe connected to the far wall. I walk over to the wall and press my ear to it. I hear the churning of large machines.

Those footsteps are on the other side of the hallway now. I turn and run, pulling her with me. I corner the hallway, and I see flashes of light behind double doors with double glass plated windows; I tug her with me, running in the opposite direction. We run past the living quarters, past the room with the tank, and corner the other hallway. At the end of that hallway is the door to the outside. Under normal circumstances, that door is locked, like every door around here is, normally. But whatever Riley did, she opened everything. I pull her along running, faster and faster. When we get to the end of the corridor, I throw myself into the doors and they fly open with ease, I'm welcomed by the chill of night. A halogen lit parking lot, several cars, one road; completely surrounded by what appears to be endless forest. Southstone is literally in the middle of nowhere. I stand on the large concrete stairs looking around, Riley pulls on my arm, but I don't move, even when I see the bouncing light of flashlights behind me.

"Come on. They're coming."

"I'll hold them off. Run straight-ahead, keep to the road, but you have to go now. Run..."

She pulls me, violently shaking her head in disagreement.

"...Run!"

She takes off from the stairs as I turn around and face the flashlights. I cover my eyes looking past the light, trying to see who holds the flashlights. It's the twins and two people I recognize as retrievers. Where is Sketch?

I'm frozen by the sound of a shotgun. Time slows as I spin to see Riley falling to her knees. From behind a car Sketch proudly walks, throwing a shotgun over his shoulder. He spits his gum and struts toward her,

"Where the fuck do you think you're going?"

I run from where I'm standing, I slide on the asphalt and catch her as she falls backward. I press my hand on her chest which is now mangled by a double zero buckshot and those nine pellets have torn her front to mauled flesh that limply hangs on the wounds, grated. The blood runs out; I can't stop the bleeding. She pants, trying to gain air from being winded but the choking worsens as blood fills her lungs. She looks up at me, choking, coughing fresh viscous scarlet on my face, painting it with splatter. She pulls at my hair so hard it hurts as she tries to speak all while her body violently convulses in my arms.

My face twists from unconcerned to empathetic. I show her I didn't mean for this to happen, and that I'm sorry. She coughs more blood and pulls me to her face and with a final forced breath she speaks,

"Hope... I hope...what you...what you found...was...worth it."

She stops moving. My muscles tremor and I'm overwhelmed, I try to fight these feelings, and I try to fight the guilt so Sketch and the others don't see, but this time, this time I can't. I can't hide how I feel. I feel hands pull at me as the twins and the retrievers try and lift me and when they do, I lose control. This is the moment I lose all control. I let go of the fear of exposure and I embrace the very thing eating at me. They will know what they did or at least they'll feel it, whether I remember it or not, I'll make them remember this moment, and I do.

As the twins grab my arms, I let them lift me and as I rise, I step behind them using the force of them, lifting me to throw them into each other. I turn and duck a Maglite flash light, meant to incapacitate me. I force my fist into the retriever Adams apple, the one who swung at me, and now he can't breathe. Through that hit I pull him, spinning, tossing him into his partner. As they fall, I recover the Maglite just as the twins recover, standing in union and when they see me, they both move as one; but I just guide the Maglite into the face of the one on the left. He falls hard as the one on the right strikes me in the jaw. I take the hit, drop the Maglite, and with both hands grab him by the throat, running him through the two retrievers. We land hard on the ground, and I begin to choke. Both retrievers throw kicks into me, but I don't budge. I just continue the pressure to his throat, squeezing and squeezing. I shake off his strikes to my face and body. I shake off more kicks from the retrievers. I continue to squeeze and squeeze, waiting for him to go limp, or to feel a pop or a crack. Something breaks my concentration, and it isn't the assault from everyone kicking me and punching me, it is the barrel of Sketch's shotgun pressed against my forehead.

"Hey! Greyor! What the fuck are you doing? Get off of him! Imagine what this will do to your face? Probably the same thing it did to that bitch's chest."

I rise, releasing the twin I had in the choke. Sketch's shotgun follows me till I'm standing. Sketch smiles.

"What the fuck is with you and that girl?"

I stand without expression, without motion, I stand absolutely still with her blood that now dries on my face and chest. I don't take my eyes off Sketch, who in kind doesn't take the shotgun off me.

"Greyor...Greyor...what am I going to do with you?"

I effortlessly shrug, tilting my head from the shotgun barrel.

"Come on Grey, talk to me, honestly. What the hell is so important about her?"

He removes the shotgun and pokes her lifeless corpse trying to get a rise from me but all I do is watch.

"Yeah, that is what I thought. Take Greyor to his room, I'll deal with him later. I'll clean her up. Go check on Hanson and while you're there, turn the fucking power back on."

The retrievers grab me and as the twins walk by, I bark,

"Now I can tell you two fuckers apart."

The twins don't acknowledge me, but Sketch does. I don't look at Sketch, but I can feel his eyes on me, and I know he is uncomfortable by my concern, because of my involvement. Sketch pokes me with his shotgun and nods at my retrievers to move me. They drag me back inside as I go limp. I think about Riley, I think about how I failed her, I think about the tank, and I think about Ian Hane. I know what it means. I know what my pills are made from. They are made from whatever they're taking from Ian Hane. That thought alone has me paralyzed and I let them pull the dead weight of my distant body as they drag me to my chamber, or as I like to call it, my prison.

BRANDON CAIN PART 2

Remember what the night sounds like? How quiet and concealed it can be? I told you to listen, if you're like Brandon you still don't. Why would you? To you, everything is fine. Everything is working out, finally. The thing is, about Brandon and Becky; they have more than me to worry about. They have to worry about the people Brandon owes money to and not so surprisingly, the people he didn't pay back. They don't even know I'm a threat. I intend to keep it that way. That is the fun thing about intentions; like I said, they are better left being intended.

As always, I come with the mask of night. People pay less attention at night. People go out less at night unless, like me, they have a purpose. Night is the place where we leave things to do last. This is how I intend to prevail, like most of my policies. I get in. I do the job, I get out. Simple enough, by now you know. Things are never simple, not even in the slightest. Especially this policy, and I can't determine why.

Like last time everything is quiet as I walk on through his neighborhood. I only recognize a problem when I get within earshot of his house. I hear Becky screaming and I hear several other voices that I'm unfamiliar with, also screaming. Three other men are screaming. I can only assume one of them is Brandon. I come from a walkway between the houses and from across the parking lot I can see a struggle. The struggle takes place right in front of Brandon's house. I see Becky on the porch, screaming, I see one man holding another while the other man beats on the man being held. I watch fist after fist find its place on his body. Cracking and crushing with each blow. As I walk up and know I still haven't been noticed, I realize they have been going on Brandon for some undetermined amount of time; long enough to do significant damage. Tissue laceration, severe bruising, a lot of bleeding, probably a cracked rib, and maybe some broken teeth. Brandon limply hangs, only standing with the help of one guy, as the other guy just lays into him, again, and again. All the while Becky screams at them to stop, he's had enough, leave him alone, someone help. That screaming may have been cut off by one of them slapping her and she may have shut up for a time but now she's back at it.

"Hey."

I make my presence known. Becky looks over and smiles.

"Johnny?"

There it is again.

The one beating on Brandon stops, looks at his partner, and then looks back at me,

"Fuck off buddy, this ain't your problem."

"No, you're right, it isn't."

I take a couple steps forward.

The guy walks toward me,

"Well then get the fuck out of..."

I lunge at him, hammering my fist into his throat and as he collapses toward me, choking. I knee him in the face. As he cracks backward, I catch him by the shirt with my left hand pulling him into my right hand, which now looks as if it will enter from one side of his skull and exit through the other. I follow through so hard I take a row of teeth out with my fist. I let him go and as he falls, I don't speak or take my time, I separate Brandon from that guy's partner. Brandon falls limply as I catch the arm of the partner who attempts to draw a gun.

I grab the arm that goes to draw the gun, his USP .45 caliber. I push down against his arm so his hand bends at the wrist holding the pistol and with my other hand I force his elbow to touch his opposite shoulder, sickly popping it out of place. He yelps but before he can deal with that horrible feeling, I throw my foot hard against the inside of his knee, causing him to buckle as his kneecap pops. He crumbles to the ground as I step over him to pick up Brandon, but before I do, I look up to hear a car door open.

"Who the fuck are you?"

I look up and over at a man dressed in a very expensive suit walking out of a very expensive car. A Mercedes, silver, glistening in the night, parked just out of sight from where I had been walking up.

"Doesn't matter."

"Yes, it does. You just fucked up two of my men who are only doing what I pay them to do. The guy you're helping owes me money, ok? Are you going to pay...?"

He walks toward me pulling a gun from his jacket.

"...Because someone has too. Maybe she will?"

As he turns to look at Becky and as he finishes his sentence, he begins to point the gun but he isn't aiming and something overtakes me. I drop to one knee, and I have my suppressed M1911A1 in hand. In three near-silent hisses, each split seconds apart, three oozing cavities now join the number of orifices he already has. One bullet goes in several millimeters above his right eyebrow, the second several inches below his neckline, and the third several millimeters below that. He doesn't even have the life left to look back to me. He falls like a string-less marionette.

"Get Brandon inside."

"Why are you doing this? You just...I mean...he is...dead...who are..."

"Becky! Get Brandon inside now!"

This is bad. I have no idea why I just did that.

Because, who else is going to, you know what they were going to do to Becky and Brandon, don't you?

What do you think I'm going to do?

Honestly, I don't know now, you're full of surprises today.

I walk over to the boss and drag him over to the Mercedes. I let him fall near the driver's side as I pop the trunk. I drag him back to the trunk and toss him in.

I walk back over to the two thugs. With gun in hand, slowly approaching the one who is most aware, slowly aiming at his skull and as he realizes I'm coming back he speaks.

"Please...man...please don't kill me man...I have a family...please man...I'll walk away, ok?"

He is on his knees begging as I get closer.

"Give me your gun."

I say it quietly and calmly. Aiming with one hand and extending the other hand with an open palm, expecting his gun. He pulls it with his useable arm from his jacket and throws it at me. His friend groggily groans on the ground with no intention of moving. His gun takes .45 caliber bullets. I pop my clip feeding the remaining four bullets into my hand while holding his gun under my arm. I put my bullets in my pocket, and I put my gun away and take his in hand, popping his clip, feeding his bullets into my hand. I take my bullets out of my pocket and feed his cartridge with them. I walk back to the trunk and fire the remaining bullets into the boss. I walk back over to him and toss him his empty gun, I lean down and help him to stand, holding him by his collar. I can see the fear in his face, and I start to whisper.

"Get the fuck out of here, and whatever you do, don't fucking come back, do you understand? You take that car and your buddy and don't come back. I don't care what you do with the body but just don't come back here, understand?"

"Who the fuck are you man?"

"Johnny. My name is Johnny. And trust me…"

Again, and again.

I look back at the car and then back to him.

"…do not make me regret this."

He nods, limping to his friend, helping him to the car. I watch them get in. I feed the bullets from his gun into my clip and then return it to my gun. I put my gun back in its holster and walk up to Brandon's door. I stand on the porch for several minutes. Just as I go to knock, the door opens. Becky stands behind the screen, staring at me. I look to the gorgeous glass heart that hangs between those beautiful tits and then I look back at her and I smile. She isn't happy to see me. I'm not sure if it is fear, or anger, or confusion, but I don't think it is happiness.

"What're you doing? The police are coming. Listen,

thank you, I mean that, but you have to go before the cops get here."

"They aren't coming."

"What?"

"Becky. They just beat the shit out of your boyfriend for how long? Nobody came then, why would they come now?"

"Because you just killed that guy!"

"And what do you think they were going to do to you?"

She just stares at me, and I just stare back.

"What do you want Johnny?"

Don't you love the sound of that?

"I need to talk to you and Brandon."

She looks at me hesitantly. Staring at me, trying to reason with herself to send me away, but somewhere inside she wants to hear what I have to say. If she owes me anything, she owes me the chance to talk, to explain what I'm doing here and why I protected them—which I still don't know —because I'm not here to protect Brandon, I'm here to kill him. I don't even know what I'm going to say but at this point I'll just speak and see what comes out. I'm as interested as she is to find out why, as why always becomes important. You know the saying curiosity kills the cat, I think curiosity does more than just kill the cat, it erases any existence of it entirely.

Becky sighs, already regretting, and opens the door. I walk in nonchalantly, smiling. I walk down a hallway into the living room where Brandon sits up regaining consciousness. He looks up at me trying to smile,

"You're Johnny?"

"Yep."

I sit down across from him.

"Thank you, man, seriously...thank you."

I nod, looking around.

"Don't."

"Are you kidding me? Those guys...they would've...I mean...if you didn't show up...they would've..."

I cut him off.

"Yeah. I know. They would've hurt Becky...but they wouldn't have killed you...just hurt you so badly that you wish you were dead...they want their money...but now, now, they don't want anything."

He looks at me, trying to hide his suspicion.

"Why are you doing this?"

"Do you really want to know?"

"Yes. You saved my life man. You didn't let anything happen to Becky. I mean, you have to want something?"

"It isn't what I want."

"What?"

"Grim associations."

"My insurance company?"

"Yeah. Your insurance company. I work for them."

"What...that doesn't make any sense...what do you do..."

I interrupt him.

"I make clients death look like accidents... but they aren't accidents. Grim associations gets paid and they pay out. To Becky. She's your beneficiary, right?"

"What? Yeah, she's my...wait, you're here to kill me? Why are you telling me this?"

Because you're done with them.

"Because I'm done with them."

"Whoa, wait, what?"

I sit forward, my gaze unflinching from Brandon, I don't even pay any attention to Becky and her wonderful body as she circles us.

"Brandon, they want me to take your life, they want that money from your life to go to Becky and a large portion to go to them because you didn't pay attention to the fine print. You lose your life and then she gets to live rich for a while until they kill her too because she accepted the money, or at least I assume that is how it is going to happen. You need to take Becky and disappear. Do you understand? Don't argue. Pack up and leave tonight."

"What? I don't understand...how can they get away with it...? How do you do this? I could call the cops...I mean they could...they have to know?"

"Brandon...you call the cops and tell them what? What have I just told you? They aren't going to believe a damn word, especially from you. Brandon, are you actually going to sit here and try and justify this? It is your choice...when really, you shouldn't even have one...I could kill you and Becky...right now...and I could make it look like an accident or make it look like you killed Becky and then killed yourself...no one would ever know. Then that money would all go to Grim...You're chosen for a reason. No family. No one cares except Becky. That is why you are insured. The life you live. No one asks questions. I mean really, really take a look at your life. Do you think anyone would actually insure you and all your asinine endeavors? You're a liability. No company in their right mind would insure you, but Grim associations would because they benefit and benefit largely. You, like many others, have always been just that, the way you live, the way you choose to live is the way we do business. One day you'll die, earlier than you should and it could be from our hands but it could just be the way you choose to live. The result will always, definitely, be the same, and for that I'm not sorry. It is your choice and finally you have it, laid neatly out in front of you; make the right one. Run away and don't come back."

"Ok...Johnny...ok...we will...I promise..."

I look at him, expressing with one look just how much I'm not fucking around.

"...I promise. We will disappear."

I smile. Relieved for the first time in a long time. I believe, for the first time in a long time, he'll make the right choice. If he doesn't, I know, I'll come back and this conversation will be irrelevant, but I can hope. *No need for hope*. I value that I can in this one moment— bad business or not—give him a choice, and I did, whether he takes it or not isn't on me.

I smile at him. I smile at Becky who is now terrified by me. Without the ability to look at me, as though I'm sick and just from glancing at me she will catch what I have, as though I'm a disease. I shrug and stand. Wiping myself off because for the first time in yet another long time, I feel honest, actually honest, like I have done right in all the wrong I have committed, if that is even possible. I smile another big fake smile and head for the door because I know I can only bask in this for a short time before Grim associations finds out and then, well then, I don't know but what I do know is I feel really good right now.

I walk down the hallway toward the front door, and I feel my phone vibrate. I stop and pull it out of my pocket. The number is blocked; I answer the call pulling the phone to my ear,

"Grey…"

"Yeah, who's this?"

"Grey…its Silk. I need you to come get me man…please…you have to come get me…"

His voice is all but shattered, he sounds weak and stuffy, as though he's been crying.

"Are you ok?"

"No man…I'm not…come get me out of here…"

"Where are you?"

"I'll send you my location…Grey?"

"Yeah, Silk?"

"Hurry."

A text message pops up, I click on it, and it gives me a location. I use my GPS to map it out. Right as I go to walk out the door, Becky calls my name.

"Johnny."

I stop and turn around.

"Thank you."

I look at her and smile honestly and then I shake my head grinning.

"Don't worry about it."

"Are you going to be, ok?"

"I don't think so."

"Why are you really helping us?"

She walks toward me with her hands at her sides, that beautiful necklace swaying with each step. She stops in front of me and fixes my collar.

"I really don't know."

"Who was that on the phone?"

"A friend."

"I know I don't know you. But I can see it in your eyes, you're in pain, and you don't want to do this, and you don't have to. Like you said to Brandon, it is all about a choice...you can choose not to do this anymore."

"Becky, I don't know anything else..."

"What do you mean?"

"I can't remember a life before this, before I started working for them, I don't know anything else and that is largely why I continue doing this, to find out, but I never remember enough of anything. I know I had a life before this, but I just don't know who I use to be..."

She cuts me off.

"You are who you are...remember it or not...you're helping us because you're drawn to it as though you wish someone would've helped you the way you helped us. Maybe that is where you should start, figuring out why you'd want to help us."

I smile.

"I have to go, and you guys should too, before they find out what I did."

She grabs my face and innocently kisses me.

"Thanks Johnny..."

She grabs the glass heart necklace, and she goes to lift it off as though she is going to give it to me.

"What're you doing? No."

I stop her.

"I want you to have it. You saved our lives. Brandon can always make another. He'll understand. Plus, it'll help you remember that you still have a heart in there."

"No, that is yours. Thank you. But you and Brandon staying alive will be thanks enough. I appreciate it but I have to go, take care of each other."

She sighs, pulling the necklace back over her neck, letting it fall back between her breasts glimmering in the light of the hallway. She looks at me, watching me, watch her.

"Thank you, Johnny. It would hurt to part with it. It was the best Valentine's gift I ever got. Brandon told me, when he gave it to me, it was the only thing more beautiful than me..."

She laughs.

"...I never take it off."

"Valentine."

"Yeah, Valentine's Day. You know, the one day dedicated to love, hallmark or not, it is still the most romantic day of the year."

"Valentyne."

"Yeah, Johnny, Valentines Day...I know this is a

stupid question, but are you ok?"

You can't ignore that. Don't ignore that. You heard it.

My hand finds the pill bottle in my pocket, but I don't remove it, instead I roll it around in my pocket.

"I have to go. Leave tonight."

I reach past Becky into the hall closet and grab a coat hanger tearing it from the bar it lives on. I look at her in the eye, just a glance, stopping in front of her face and I smile a wide smile, winking.

She flashes me with a smile, and I walk out the front door to her speaking,

"What is that for?"

I don't look back.

"Hanging stuff on, shirts, jackets, even dresses…"

I turn mid-walk and smile.

"…Or in my case, opening stuff."

I leave Becky and Brandon there. They are on their own. I'm not coming back.

That a boy. Focus. Focus on the name.

I reach at the pills.

Stop running.

As I walk, I keep going to reach for them, but I never take them out. I lift them and drop them inside my pocket.

Concentrate.

I have to get to Silk.

No, not that, on y...

I inhale deeply walking back to the other side of the parking lot, Brandon's house is far enough that I can't hear them if they called my name. I begin to bend the coat hanger as I look at the parked vehicles. I look around. Investigating, seeing if anyone is around, and when I don't see or hear anyone I start to decide. Which vehicle do I take? Which vehicle do I want to take?

Out of many options, only one stands out.

A black GMC Sierra. A black, turbo diesel, GMC Sierra. I can open the door without breaking a window and I can hot-wire it. It doesn't have an alarm. I can open that locked door with this simple metal coat hanger, and I won't break anything. I can't promise the same for the wiring. I can open that door in a minute flat and have the truck started in maybe another minute and I can be driving away in the next minute. Three minutes is a very short time. Some can do it faster but stealing cars or trucks isn't my specialty. Then again three minutes can seem a lot longer when you need to be somewhere.

I slip the coat hanger where window meets windshield. I let the hook grab the lip of the door lock. I pop it up. I get in removing the coat hanger and quietly shut the door. I flip out the blade of my pocketknife and I pop out the ignition switch from the dash and unplug it. I find the main hot wire, which is red with a yellow stripe, and I find its black partner with a green stripe. I splice them. I take the motor crank wire and touch it to them and when the motor starts, I remove the crank wire. I put my foot on the brake, throw the truck into reverse and roll back from between two parked cars. I don't speed off. I drive away slowly over the many speed bumps that litter the parking lot. I open my phone and pull up the GPS and map watching myself head toward Silks location.

It has been a while since I've taken my pills. I want to. I want this to stop. The madness of trying to reconnect to what I've lost. Every moment I spend trying to remember things before this life and in every moment that passes, I don't. When I don't, something opens inside. I start to feel but do not remember. I'm feeling things I haven't felt in a very long time. Things I haven't felt since I woke up in a hospital bed in Southstone. Things like remorse, pity, desire, and finally, loss. From what, I don't know. In the mix, I get angry, I feel betrayed and again I don't know why.

These emotions I'm having distract me sometimes from what is important: staying alive, the only thing keeping me going is to do just that. I'm surviving. I always feel as though I'm in danger, as if at any moment something bad is about to happen, and when it doesn't, I still don't find comfort. I'm constantly at unease. I analyze everything around me. I look for things that aren't there. The medication stops that. But it also pushes something inside away. Something inside that desperately wants out. That is my only constant; the feeling that someone wants to get out, as though I've trapped someone else inside me.

I assume—even when I should know—that trapped person is who I used to be. My identity, screaming up at me to stop, stop what I'm doing, stop it before I hurt someone else, but I don't listen. Those pills help me ignore him. He knows what I'm doing is wrong. He wants to drive but I don't let him. I don't let him drive, because then you wake up in a hospital bed and you don't remember how you got there but you have an instinctual concept that you may not want to know how you got there.

You are there for a reason. Then people constantly cement the idea that what you did is something unforgivable, something wrong, but they never tell you what it is because it won't help you get "better". They keep telling you that they want you to get better, want to help you get better, but these people torture you, and they train you.

You know you're not getting better even when you don't know what better is.

They teach you things that scare you at first and then suddenly you can't stop wanting to know more.

They teach you how to stay out of that hospital bed.

They teach you how to withstand large amounts of pain and to defend yourself from multiple people trying to injure you, or worse, kill you. They teach you how to shoot a gun and use a knife and then when you ask questions, they torture you and dose you with medication that they say will help you remember, but it never does. You begin to just function without knowing much of anything like who you are, how you got to where you are in one moment, or how you got back from where you were in the next, or even what you did in the last, but you hold on to pieces. People you've killed and how you killed them. You live in the moment and only the moment and it sounds a lot better than it is.

Then one day, sitting in a hotel or motel or whatever that fucking place was, you start feeling something, something foreign, and you stop functioning without knowing all those things and that is when they begin to suspect you. You don't remember who you were, but you remember what you've been doing and suddenly, you want to stop doing it and that is when they begin to test you.

When they get you out of that bed and they drag you down a corridor and shock you, you start to fake it; pretend you don't remember. Or wake you up in a courtyard where people try to kill you, and the only way you're getting out is to kill everyone else. When you don't remember who you are, you know that whoever you were really wanted to stay alive because you woke up from something that should've killed you. If that happens, you base everything on staying alive.

You stay alive because you have something before this. A name before Greyor...All black...you don't remember it because you can't, doesn't mean you won't. However, you won't remember if you keep taking those pills. Those pills help you stay Grey or all black or nothing at all. You had a life before this. Those people's lives that you take, someone took yours, go get it back, you didn't give them that option.

I gave Becky and Brandon one.

Why?

I don't know.

Yes, you do.

Because she stays with him. It doesn't matter what he does. She stays.

And why does that matter? I mean, what about Helena, she had a family.

I don't know why I killed her. I mean I didn't. She jumped.

She didn't know you'd be there with a rock.

I feel something powerful grip at my throat, choking me.

Let it happen.

I shake violently, coughing, accelerating. I don't want to feel this.

Yes, you do.

She didn't deserve to die. I should've dropped the rock but if they found out I did, if she lived, they would've killed me.

They can't kill you. You won't let that happen. They've tried. How do you think you got in that hospital bed?

Someone shot me in the head.

It was an accident. You need to remember that. It was a fucking accident. She was trying to protect you. Don't fucking blame her.

My head hurts and images play through my head in no particular order, but something sticks even though I don't understand it.

She left me there...to die. They were coming and she left me there to die.

That's not how it happened. You need to remember all of it. She didn't leave you...

I've reached my destination. Outside a house my GPS icon connects perfectly to Silks location. I look over at the house, all the lights are off, and I don't see anyone moving. I know this house. I've been here before. This is Alexander Burish's house. I put the truck into park, disconnect the wires. It dies quietly in the night.

HOW WE GET AWAY WITH THE BAD THINGS WE DO

Next time you pick up a newspaper I want you to count the number of deaths you read about. How someone died: got hit by a car or died in a crash; fell off a building; went for a swim; died in a fire or died from smoke inhalation; died of a drug overdose or died of what would appear to be natural causes. Sometimes this just happens, people just die, but sometimes it's me and the people I work with making it look like those times. I'm not saying that if somebody had been looking for a murder, they wouldn't find it. It's a matter of looking and how hard. Appearances are everything when it comes to an investigation. They call it foul play when they don't know what happened and it just looks like a death, but a suspicious one. Even when the death is suspicious or looks like foul play it all depends on who died. People pay attention to tragedy. People don't give a fuck about a drug addict overdosing because it is more likely to happen, so, people don't care. Gang members get gunned downed, again, this will happen. Someone in security getting shot, again, it is more likely to happen then not. Case closed. Now, if the person is a saint or appears to be a saint and do not fucking say law is blind because she isn't the bitch has one eye open, and she sees what she wants to see. If a person who is loved by many dies and foul play is suspected, the investigation is generally more thorough. It is not playing; it is not a game. It is life turning to death and I am the one turning it.

So, for appearance's sake we usually make it look like an accident or make it look natural, but it all comes down to how our policy is ensured and what for. I'd been wondering why no one investigates, especially when, for instance: someone shoots at a security detail from a bus. There was an investigation, but it led them after the enemies of the diplomat, not who was actually responsible for murdering Alexander. Now, if someone had been paying really close attention, they would have noticed the money going to Alexander's wife. But that is the entire point of life insurance. Someone dies. Someone gets money. What is there to investigate?

Obviously, someone could unravel this entire operation if they started looking into how everyone died, but they wouldn't, because most of time, everything—well, usually everything—resembles an accident.

Speaking of Alexander.

You remember Alexander Burish, of course you do. I can`t forget him, any of them. Not one of them. I tried to, I gave it an honest go, but I couldn't. Even with the pills. All the medication did was drown out how I felt but it didn't remove their existence. I had a hand at destroying not just each person, but everyone connected to them, even though that isn't many people. Remember, each client is chosen because they have very little connections left; that of a family, and as it turns out, we remove those as well.

For example, Alexander had a girlfriend, Emily. I say had because, well, he's dead, and now so is she. As I walk into their bedroom, I see her on the bed and I don't need to investigate closely, check for a pulse, because from where I'm standing, I can tell she's dead and somehow this feels familiar. This room has been turned over, the night side tables are knocked over face down, the closet has been tossed, clothes litter the floor, broken pictures and broken glass decorated soil and broken pottery amongst the pile of laundry. Amongst the clutter and destruction, Silk sits, leaning up against the opposite side of the bed, opposite to the door to this room, his back is to me. From the minute I entered the house I could smell cigarettes and here he is smoking a cigarette, drinking from a twenty six ounce bottle of whisky. I can't tell what brand because someone has peeled the label off, I say someone, because I'm not sure if it was him. The blinds have been torn from their brackets half-hanging over the window and from the window I can see Silks reflection, his face, he is staring up at me through the reflection. I can see a blurry reflection of my shadow in the door frame, leaning against it, looking around before turning my face back and staring at the reflection, staring back at Silk.

"Hey Grey. Thanks for coming."

"What happened in here?"

"I did."

"You did this? Did you kill her?"

"She fucked up the room...she was upset...she..."

I step forward interrupting him, almost lunging toward him stopping at the corner of the bed as he speaks, and I get a better look at her. She has no wounds. Nothing I can see. No blood. No tissue damage. No signs of a struggle but in no way does it look like she died peacefully. I don't look at her, I look back to him.

"I thought you..."

"What, rape her? I don't have too. I never have to force myself, anywhere, on anyone. They let me do what I want. They can't help themselves. I thought I fucking told you this Grey, or did you forget? Did you take more of that..."

I cut him off.

"I remember. You're poisonous."

He looks up at me, his eye sockets stung red from

pulling at the skin when he wipes his face clean. Flushed, his eyes bloodshot surrounded by rose circles under each eye. But when he looks up at me his cheeks pull tight to dimples and he momentarily looks happy, smiling.

"You fucking remember? Awe Grey, I'm proud of you...so fucking...so fucking...proud."

He whimpers choking out his voice. He stops talking to drink down a few gulps of that whisky as he extinguishes his cigarette on the floor.

"What happened Silk?"

I kneel down, right beside him. I place my hands on my knees and arch my back, cracking it. With a sick crack I'm relieved and I turn my attention back to him. Speechlessly, he stares at himself in the window. He goes to raise his bottle to his lips but turns suddenly as he looks to me and questions my actions as I go into his coat and remove his smokes. I pull one out and place it in his lips. I grab his Zippo which lies next to his hand and flick it open effortlessly and roll the wheel and give fire to the end of his cigarette. He breathes in slowly, removing the cigarette, and downs another several gulps of his whisky. He then he blows the smoke he had in his lungs before, staring back at himself.

"Thanks."

"No problem."

"Hey Grey?"

I sit down next to him.

"Yeah?"

"Do you remember who you were?"

"No."

"But you remember everything else?"

"I remember everything—well, mostly everything—since I woke up. Nothing before that though, why?"

"It must be nice."

"What?"

"Well, I remember everything...every last fucking one...and even before I got paid...I can remember every girl and how they tasted. What they looked like...before...and after. I don't know why I still do it..."

He coughs.

"...maybe I do it because I want one...just one...too

He closes his eyes, crying silently before inhaling heavily to fight the sadness, to find control.

"...live. So maybe I'll be close to someone longer than a night. So, I can feel like they do...I just want...you know...to have someone...but every time..."

He points to Emily.

"...every single time. I drive them crazy. They give me whatever I ask. It should feel amazing but look..."

He points to Emily.

"...That happens every fucking..."

He chokes, takes a drag and then gulps another couple of shots of whisky.

"...time. I kill them."

"I don't know Silk. At least you make them happy, even though momentary, they are happy?"

He laughs.

"Does that fucking look happy?"

He points to Emily, and I turn my head and look at her from over my shoulder. She is pale and cold. Her eyes decline pigment for a sick white glaze. She has dark film encrusting the border of her lips. Her hair is damp and twisted, mangled into the bed sheets. Her skin is tight and clammy. Silk is right, she doesn't look like she died happily. Something about all of this is familiar.

"Does the company know about this? About Christina?

I turn and look back to Silk.

Silk takes another drag, looking at me.

"No. They don't."

I nod. Looking back at the reflection of Silk plastered on the window, I'm just out of the reflection.

"I did something I shouldn't have Silk."

"What?"

"I let someone live and I told him what I was going to do."

"Grey? Why...why would you do that man...I told

you…play along."

"I don't know…it isn't working for you Silk."

"Who was it?"

"Brandon Cain."

"Again? Why don't you just kill him? You don't hesitate. Since I've met you, you go after the policy; pure business. You fill it and then the retrievers bring you back…if Sketch finds out…I don't know Grey. Not trying to offend you but someone else can do what you do…if they find out about me…I don't know…but what I've done for them and what I continue to do is irreplaceable. Sorry to say, but you're replaceable."

I smile.

"Thanks Silk."

"I said no offense. But Grey…. you're trouble and nothing but and you…"

He takes a long-winded breath inward.

"…have been since they picked you up…I never understood why…other than you being the biggest pain in the ass…"

"Silk?"

"Yeah Grey?"

"I want you to tell me about the company, how it works, tell me about Sketch?"

"Why?"

I grab his smokes and Zippo, I take one out and throw it effortlessly in my mouth and with the other hand I flick the Zippo lid open and light it sucking back so deeply it burns. I let smoke trickle from my nose as I look back to him.

"Just tell me."

He smiles, chuckles, grabs his smokes and his Zippo back and joins me. He takes a couple of swigs from the bottle and exhales heavily, so heavily it sounds painful.

"Do you know what becomes of a man when you strip him of hope? But not just hope, all things he looked forward to, loved, and held close to his heart. The very things that allow him strength to survive day after day, after day of the never ending misery of the mundane?"

"No?"

"You get Benjamin Sketch. He lost the very things that kept him from collapse. Everything he loved, and I mean every single last thing he loved and built, was taken from him, all in one day, in the span of fifteen minutes. That is how he became the way he is, it is sad, really, because of that fifteen minutes and I know it sounds cliché, but he was never the same. He once was a loving husband and very proud father..."

"Sketch?"

"...Yes. Sketch. He had a home, a dog, a nice car, lived in a friendly neighbourhood, and even had a well manicured lawn with barbeque and patio set up. In his mind, he had everything, everything he ever wanted, with the exception of a job that didn't take every last second of his attention. Every one of those seconds created one more minute less he had to spend with the things and people he loved.

His wife, and no..."

Silk stops and looks at me.

"...I don't remember her name. She always wanted him to be there for her and for their daughter. But again, to Sketch, he had to be at this job..."

"What did he do?"

Silk laughs loudly, blowing a plume of smoke from the side of his mouth before continuing.

"Insurance claims investigator. He loved his job. It helped him get all those things he loved: the dog, the nice car, the lawn with the patio set. Over the years Sketch saw things, things that even the goriest horror flick couldn't depict. This caused him to lose a lot of sleep, which surprisingly, caused him to work more. I don't know why, and he didn't either, but it did. So slowly Sketch began to see less and less of his family— and I know Grey—I know that you're waiting for this line...until one day.

Sketch had been investigating a series of claims, strange deaths, all similar and all had the same cause of death. The cause of death appeared like a drug overdose..."

I smile,

"You?"

"Sadly, yes, he was the first person to see it..."

"The first?"

"...I will get to that. Sketch sat up, night after night, going through the files, the photos, the evidence, and policy legislation. He drank cold coffee and smoke cigarette after cigarette. He had been awake for just about thirty-six hours and all he wanted to do was shut his eyes...until he saw it. Not exactly what he had been looking for, but something stood out. Two of his last four policies had me as their beneficiary. They both died the same way, as did all four he'd been investigating, and the connection, despite that none should exist, was right there in front of his tired eyes. There it was, a mathematical impossibility, too convenient to be a coincidence, and to his shock, I worked for his company. The whole time he'd been investigating the deaths, when really, he should be investigating his company. Sketch found the last identifiable mistake Grim associations would ever make on paper and that same day, Sketch lost his life.

Benjamin Sketch lost everything that made him remotely human on December fourteenth, nineteen ninety nine. The day his daughter disappeared and that is just coincidence, Grim had no hand in his daughter's disappearance. She was eleven years old. Her mother was supposed to pick her up at the mall, but instead, she was fucking her lover in his office. She was forty-five minutes late getting to the mall. Had she been half an hour late, she would've got there before William Hynes took her.

William Hynes was...yes...was a convicted sex offender with a taste for young girls. He had only been out of prison for two days. Samantha Sketch would become his first murder..."

"Fuck."

"...It is horrible to imagine fifteen minutes would determine the life or death of Benjamin's daughter. They never found Samantha's body, but they found her clothes shoved inside William's laundry basket. Hynes never made it back to prison. They found him mutilated under a bridge, cause of death was blood loss—his genitals had been removed—the weapon wasn't found.

Hynes became Sketch's first victim, even though Hynes wasn't a victim, but you get the point. The second victim was Sketch's wife, who committed "suicide"..."

"How?"

"...Drug overdose. Yeah, Sketch found me, told me if I didn't help him, he would expose me or kill me and really at that point I'm not sure what I was more afraid of, Sketch, exposure, or death. Sketch's wife's lover "died" in a car accident a day later. I don't know why I helped him. The company could've killed me for that, but suddenly, Sketch became one of the biggest players. This had been going on before me...before Sketch...it all started with those drugs..."

"Wait. Silk. So, Sketch didn't start this?"

"...No, he didn't, and honestly, I don't know who did, but it has been going on for awhile. Anyone that somehow finds out dies, or joins."

"I thought Sketch was the boss? I thought he ran things?"

"No, but he is a big part of it now. So am I and I hate to say this, but so are you."

"What about Hanson?"

"The doctor?"

"Yeah?"

"I don't know anything about him."

"The twins?"

"Don't know them."

"Who else? What else do you know?"

"I know that everyone we "collect" doesn't have anything really linking them to a life, no one would really miss them, and if they did, we get rid of them. I know that this all started because of those fucking meds you shovel down your throat and so do most of the people at Southstone or the others who do what you do."

"What about you?"

"Why are you so curious?"

"I don't know...for two reasons...one being I don't know what they're going to do to me when they find out what I did...the second, I want to know who my friend is."

He looks at me. His face cringes. I distracted him long enough but now every feeling that brought him to the side of the bed whimpering, whatever made him call me, rushes back.

"Grey..."

He starts whimpering.

"I'm sorry for what we did to you...I'm..."

I smile.

"It's ok Silk. Talk to me, help me understand."

"...man, you have no reason to help me...you have all the reason to kill me...why...why do you...care?"

I shrug.

"Because whatever you did...you're helping me now. That means you're risking yourself for me."

"No, Grey..."

He begins to cry, snot runs loosely and then he dries his nose with his sleeve.

"...You've had what I always wanted, and I helped them...I helped them...I know you don't remember but...Grey...you shouldn't be here."

"Silk. Tell me about you...but breathe first...it is ok."

"No Grey, it isn't...you don't know what you're

talking about...trust me...you have no idea..."

I cut him off.

"Help me understand then..."

"I told you what you needed to know about me. Everyone I touch, dies..."

He puts his face in his hands.

"...I wish I didn't do this...but I can't stop myself...it's bad enough that I help Grim with their loose ends, but I have to stop dipping in...I don't need the money...I don't want it anymore..."

"If it makes you feel any better, I don't get paid. I do this because I don't want to die."

"Neither do I Grey. I hate doing this...but death isn't an option."

"Why not just leave?"

"They'll find me, they always do, find me, like you found me. I've got nowhere else to go, nothing else to do. What about you? Why don't you just leave?"

"Same as you, I have nowhere else to go. Plus, I won't get answers leaving. I need to know who I am."

"You have somewhere else to go. I can help you get back there."

"Silk what do you know about me?"

He hands me his Zippo.

"This is yours."

I look at him, confused, denying his statement with a shake of my head.

From my peripherals I see movement outside the window. Casually, I look back at Silks reflection,

"We have to go."

"Why?"

"Retrievers."

At night they're always dressed in flat black tactical gear, bulletproof vests, black nylon masks with eye slits, and black gloves. Each one armed with taser guns intending to take my unconscious ass back to Southstone. During the day they look like normal people who wait for the opportune time to strike, large groups of people usually mask their appearance, they move quickly, collect, and leave. That is how I'm usually returned to Southstone.

"How many?"

"I don't know."

He puts his smokes in his pocket, turns the cap back on his bottle of whiskey, and looks at me.

"Have you thought about what were going to do?"

"Were going back to Southstone, you're going to show me how to get back there. I..."

"Are you fucking crazy? They're going to kill you...I'm not taking you back, we have to get..."

"...No, we have to go back. I need to know how to get back there. We can't let the retrievers take me..."

"...Grey, we can take them out and disappear, I have money but if I take you back, you're dead, and I don't want that to happen."

"…I appreciate it Silk, but I have to go back."

He shakes his head, touching his chin to his chest, and then he looks back at me.

"It's your fucking funeral."

We rise up at the same time, oddly synchronous, and walk toward the hallway to the front door, out past the kitchen and past the living room.

"Why don't we go out the back way?"

"The truck I'm using is on the street, plus the back leaves us completely open to…"

"And the front doesn't?"

"Not as bad as the back, trust me on this. If we have to go around the house to get to the truck they can come from either direction, pincer us, at least if we go through the front our back is covered, we'd hear them come through the house.

Are you ready for this?"

He nods. I put my hand on the doorknob, looking out from the side window, and I can't see them, but I know they're out there somewhere. It's funny, Alex's girlfriend didn't believe in the same level of security he did. This door isn't reinforced, which normally would be bad if I was trying to defend this location but considering I'm trying to leave, well, it is going to help with that. This is a normal wooden door, held on by brackets and screws, the door opens to the right but

I'm going to make it open to the left.

I hold on to the doorknob with my left hand and throw the entire weight of my body in one solid kick, ripping the door from its brackets. The door swings violently to the left, connecting with a retriever waiting next to the door, he falls under the door as Silk, and I take off from the porch. As we hit the grass, I tumble just as two miniature harpoons fly over me striking Silk in the chest. He drops as a current is introduced into his body from a taser in the hands of a retriever no more than ten feet from us on the side of the house, just under cover from bushes separating properties. I recover from the tumble into a dash spearing into the one electrocuting Silk. The bull rush sends him toppling over himself. I grab the taser and eject the cartridge with the nodes connected to Silk. Silk goes to stand as I grab at the downed retriever, throwing the butt end of the taser into his face, I grab an extra cartridge from his belt quickly reloading the gun, I spin, dropping to the ground on my back, firing at the retriever coming up from between my stolen truck and another car parked on the street. When the harpoons dig into the soft flesh of his neck, I don't let go of the trigger until he is on the ground, convulsing. I eject that cartridge, stand, and feed the taser a fresh one, searching for another retriever, when no one comes forth I look at Silk,

"You, ok?"

He wipes himself off, walking toward the truck, unscrewing the whisky cap and taking a quick sip before recapping it.

"I'm fine, let's just get the fuck out of here."

I power walk to the truck, opening the door and reconnecting the wires, touching the crank wire and then releasing it when it starts, as Silk sits up in the passenger seat watching me. He nudges me and nods to the retriever walking toward the truck, I toss him the taser and he rolls down the window and smiles. As the retriever goes to aim, Silk puts the electrodes into his leg with a quick well placed shot. As he drops, I go to drive away and as I do, Silk releases the taser letting it smash on the ground.

I put my foot to the accelerator, listening to the turbo hiss as the automatic transmission changes the gears for me. We peel through a neighbourhood quickly and quietly without squealing tires, trying to evade any tail, if someone is even following us. It isn't until I'm three blocks from Emily's house does Silk speak.

"Grey, why do you want to go back? When they find out you didn't kill Brandon, they're going to kill you. When they find out that you attacked a retrieval squad, they're going to kill you. From where it stands, doesn't matter what you do, they're going to kill you."

"They're going to try, Silk. That is the difference between trying and succeeding. The thing is, I need to finish this. I need to know more and I'm not going to learn anything running. I have to see this through, death or not. Like you said, they have tried and they're just going to have to try harder."

"Alright, well, for the record, I'm sorry. I really am. You're a good friend, Grey."

MY FINAL INTERROGATION

Usually when I return to Southstone I'm heavily sedated and in the back seat of a retrieval vehicle. I understand why, because it is completely and totally secluded, so far from any type of civilization the drive alone is sedating. I'd say Southstone is in the middle of nowhere but nowhere has more near it than Southstone does.

Several hours of driving, several unpaved roads that climb and climb to what appears nowhere, and finally one seemingly strangely placed, paved road takes me to the front entrance of Southstone: a facility that doesn't exist. Before I make the final stretch of road, I stop on the shoulder, only several meters from Southstone. I turn and look at Silk.

"Get out."

"What, why?"

"They can't know you helped me."

"I think it is a bit late for that."

"No, it isn't. You don't need to be part of this."

He looks at me. A smile creeps over his swollen, puffy cheeks. He polishes off his whisky, takes two smokes out and looks at me, he looks at me like it is the last time he is going to see me. I pass him the Zippo and he lights them, and he passes me one. He hands me the Zippo. I take it and sit back smoking slowly, letting every breath sit and still in my lungs before exhaling slowly.

"Hey Grey?"

"Yeah Silk?"

"Thank you."

"For what?"

"For helping me. I mean, I may not be out yet, but if you don't know who the fuck you are and you are still trying to get out of this. I can to."

I smile, finishing my cigarette, tossing it out the window. I look back at him and smile.

"You never know, you may find someone you who kiss doesn't die. I mean, it is possible. Anything is. I'd feel sorry for the girl who has to live through that but, you know, fingers crossed."

He laughs.

"Get out Silk."

He smiles and opens the door, stepping out, tossing his cigarette he looks at me,

"Good luck."

I smile and put the truck back into drive and gun it for the entrance. I slide around the horseshoe roadway entrance and slam on the breaks sliding into the stone staircase. I throw the truck into park and disconnect the wires, killing the truck. I step out to the sound of

Sketch's voice.

"Grey, what the fuck?"

I look over to him, standing in the doorway smoking a cigarette, puzzled by my entrance, by my lack of company.

"Sketch."

I nod.

He takes a deep breath, shaking his head.

"How the fuck did you get here?"

"I remembered. It's funny. I mean, one second, I'm at Brandon's, and in the next, I'm on the way back here."

I walk toward Sketch.

His expression blanks, his gaze goes cold, and his relaxed frame goes stiff. As I climb the stairs he doesn't move. He just stares at me, his expression almost disappointed. As I reach for the doors, I feel two electrodes penetrate my skin and I feel powerful current cripple my joints and overwhelm my strength. I fall to my knees as I barely turn my attention to Sketch and the taser that is now in his hands. He firmly holds down the trigger as I fall in front of his feet. He leans down still pressing the trigger. The current is debilitating to the point I can't even turn to look at him, and he whispers,

"This isn't a fucking game."

I lose consciousness.

I wake to freezing water soaking my bare skin. My eyes open and I'm so groggy it is nauseating. I'm strapped firmly to a metal chair bolted to the floor. I have lost comprehension of time, but I know I've been unconscious and sedated for several days at least. I'm in a small room. Sketch, Hanson, and the twins are my company. As I regain consciousness pains devours my nerve endings, as I look down, I barely make out the two jagged teeth clamps meant to charge car batteries attached to each ankle. I limply lift my head, so slowly; my ascent takes what little strength I have to hazily comprehend what is happening.

"Well hello Greyor."

Sketch stands grinning, holding a small metal bucket; he tosses it aside and walks over to a table.

His hand goes to a switch that is connected to some wires that are connected to a battery. More wires run from the battery to those clamps that are connected to my ankles. I close my eyes momentarily before looking back at Sketch. Hanson walks around the room. The twins stand absolutely still in front of the door. Everyone is quiet. The only noise is my breathing. I'm shivering and deeply exhaling before sucking more air back in, trying to shake off the cold to distract myself from the pain and to fight the anticipation of what is coming: more pain. My vision goes from blurry to focused, and then back to blurry.

"So, Grey, what happened with Brandon?"

"I let him live."

Sketch's grin slowly changes to a smile and then instantaneously becomes a scowl. Within the moment his brow shifts, pulling the leather of his cheeks tight on his jaw, he tosses the switch over. I hear the sound of something clinking and then the dry crank of crackling electricity muffles that noise. The lights all but die and I feel tremendous agony as a brand new pain penetrates every end of nerve I have. Every muscle simultaneously contracts; I lose control of my jaw as I bite down onto my tongue. My body gyrates uncontrollably, and I smell something, the aroma of the flesh on my ankles cooking. I can hear myself scream, but I can't stop. When the pain stops, I still feel it insubstantially. The lights come back and I'm still shaking. I spit warm blood on to my legs as I feel my tongue swell. I regain feeling in my body.

"Fu...ck..."

"Painful, isn't it? How're those ankles Grey?"

"Wh...y...are y...you...doing... th...is?"

I can't form sentences because of the swelling of my tongue and the chattering of my teeth.

"You fucking know why. You remember."

Sketch lunges at me, throwing a fist across the right side of my jaw and limply my head bounces from the arm of my chair, I hear something clink again.

"Ow."

I spit more blood, it cascades over my bottom lip painting its way down my chin, and as I watch it fall, I slowly look up at Sketch, smiling, almost laughing.

"You little mother fucker..."

He hits me again and again and again until finally when I can't see straight, he lifts my head up painfully, tugging my hair.

"What the fuck do you remember?"

He screams right into my face, his spittle blinding me.

Don't tell him.

"Everything...since I woke up in that hospital bed...I remember the training... the torture...the courtyard...the policies..."

"What fucking else?"

Hanson walks forward, disbelieving, he goes to speak but Sketch cuts him off.

"Greyor, what else?"

"Everything since I woke up...but mostly...the violence..."

He hits me hard pulling my face down toward the arm of the chair again. I begin to fade out. My mind blanks. Unconsciousness is coming. I hear that clinking again, something glass, the sound where you touch metal to glass. That millisecond hum you get as soon as you tap glass. I keep hearing it, barely, but it is there, over and over; somewhere in this room. I overhear Sketch and Hanson talking.

"You told me there was no way he could fucking remember anything, only what he was doing, you said he could only retain short-term. Did you not fucking say that?"

"I don't know why it is happening, he shouldn't have long-term memories. I have to run some tests. Check the level of medication in his blood. I'll send my findings to Alrick."

"Oh, you have to do some tests? Oh, alright..."

I hear Hanson cough, I hear the wind being knocked out of his lungs and then I hear him yelp as Sketch pulls him standing.

"Did you not fucking say he wouldn't remember?"

"Yes...I said that..."

I hear footsteps, simultaneous footsteps, the twins step forward.

"Call your dogs off or I swear I'll snap your neck."

"Its fine boys...really...I'm ok...step back."

"You want to explain something to me Doc, why did the same thing happen to that little blonde bitch? Why did she remember?"

"The new medication is having unexpected side effects..."

"Oh. Is that all? So, you're saying the new batch is completely useless?"

"In Greyor and Riley's case, yes."

"Is it Hane?"

"No, Alrick changed the medication."

"Do we still have the old stuff?"

"Yes."

"Then fucking start dosing people with the medication that does what it supposed to."

"I still need to do some blood work..."

Sketch interrupts him loudly,

"Go fucking get the old medication, right fucking now Hanson, no tests."

Hanson leaves the room. The twins follow synchronously behind.

"Fucking moron."

Sketch speaks to himself.

I fall unconscious to that clinking noise. I open my eyes and I'm looking down on a surgery table. I'm not conscious. I'm remembering. Two men are laid out on tables. Both have mutilated faces. I'm one of those men. I don't recognize the second man...

Of course you don't his face is all fucked up.

I stare down at myself. I watch in horror as my mutilated eyes click open. I hear running. Two people wrapped in medical gowns run up next to me.

"Why is he conscious?"

"I don't know, give me the anaesthetic."

One man passes the other a hypodermic needle

which is quickly pushed into an open IV in my arm. He injects it and I scream. I grab his arm tugging him.

"Why the fuck is he awake?"

I hear an alarm. The two doctors fight with me. I'm sitting up, screaming, my face open and exposed, the flesh pinned back. More doctors rush in to help restrain me. Suddenly, I fall unconscious as the doctors reposition me.

"Let just get this over with."

I lose sight of this room and the people in it. I find darkness and when I open my eyes again, I'm somewhere else. I'm still remembering.

I turn and Sketch is standing behind me grinning.

"Go ahead, take your pick."

I turn and look forward. Shelves and tables littered with weapons sit in front of me.

This is when you got your gun.

I walk, guided toward one shelf. On it, the M1911A1 pistol that eventually became *my* M1911A1 pistol. I lift it up off the shelf holding it up to the light. At that time, it was damaged, pieces need to be replaced, but this gun, like me, has survived awhile and a lot. It had survived much more than I had. It had seen both world wars, modified in the second to greet its new build and continued to keep someone alive through other wars and battles. I have no idea what parts of the world this gun had seen or who it had killed, but somehow it wound up here.

"Odd choice. Don't you want something newer?"

"No. I will get this one working again."

"I guess for you, that it is suitable."

He smacks me on the back, chuckling to himself, but I don't take my eyes off the gun as I cycle open the chamber, it always slides easily, it needs several new pieces but this part stays. I walk through the armoury collecting other .45 caliber guns, mostly 1911 clones or anything with suitable parts, and when I get everything, I need, I sit down and rebuild this gun.

As soon as I begin to assemble it, I'm stolen from this memory. Darkness returns and I'm elsewhere. This is new. I open my eyes to the sound of knocking. I feel hands on my back, and I hear unimpressed grumbling from a soft pleasant voice, I recognize it, and I find comfort just hearing it again.

"Baby, the door. Please get the door, banana."

I look to the clock. It is early. The red digits flick over to six partnered with two zeros. Six am. I sit up, crack my back, and roll my neck, fighting the urge to stay in bed despite the constant knocking of a door. I feel a hand on the small of my back, pulling my underwear waist band.

"Give me a kiss first."

I look back smiling, my eyes barely open; I crawl across the warm bed and turn her over. She has her eyes closed and her lips puckered, and she keeps opening and closing them kissing at the air. I move her tussled locks; they shine gold in the light, from her mostly blonde hair that she streaked out her original color: dark brown. I run my hands through it as I go into the kiss, soft and outside and over her lips drawing them against mine. I take my time with each return of her lips, letting her lead the kiss as I slide my hands down her waist and on to her hips, pulling her into me.

The knock gets louder.

She puts her hands on my waist. I hesitantly pull from her kiss, deeply sighing. She opens up her beautiful eyes. They shine in the soft morning glow, gorgeously transitioning to adjust to the light that glides over her pupils. That soft brown outer sun around her pupil draws the blue cerulean that finally is deeply embraced by the jade green area before the unveiling white of her fully opened eyes. Her smirk becomes a grin as she runs her hands up against my inner thighs before pulling around each cheek of my ass. She smacks me on each cheek, giggling before pushing me up.

"You better put some pants on if you're still going to answer the door, cobra."

She winks and rolls over. I groan as I sluggishly leave the warm comfort of my bed for a pair of torn jeans that are now painful to pull on. I stumble down the stairs, almost limping my way to the front door. I feel calm and relaxed and happy. I haven't felt like this…It has been so long since…I can't remember this feeling but now it is all I feel as I watch…I know this is a memory and as I watch it all but fades because I know that I'm strapped to a chair somewhere else.

I get to the door and tear it open.

"What?"

"Mr. Valentyne?"

"Yeah?"

When my eyes adjust to the light, I'm greeted by two men in suits holding brief cases.

"And who are you guys?"

"We represent Grim associations, can we come in? It is about your claim."

"Wait, what? What claim?"

"It is better if we explain it in private, it is a sensitive matter; you lost someone recently, did you not?"

"Come in."

I let them walk by me. I should be more alarmed, but in this memory I'm tired and want to go back to bed. They walk into the living room, looking around. I walk by them and fall heavily on my couch. I pull out a pack of cigarettes and a Zippo. I remove a cigarette and roll my Zippo around between my thumb and fingers and watch them circle the living room,

"Do you want to sit down? You're making me nervous."

I flick open the Zippo as they sit down across from me and take a deep inhale. The talkative one speaks up.

"Laurie Benson, did you know her?"

"Yeah, she was my ex-girlfriend...she..."

I look out the window, wincing.

"...passed away six months ago, why do you ask?"

"You were the beneficiary to her claim..."

I interrupt sharply,

"You know she overdosed right? You insure overdoses?"

"...no discernable drug was found in the post-mortem. Her cause of death was deemed natural therefore you will be reimbursed for your loss."

I hear a noise from the hallway, I'm sitting on the coach facing the hallway, and the two men face me with their backs to the door. The girl from my bed comes around the corner; her name is Jess, she stands in the doorway closing her robe, covering her naked frame, shocked to find we have company, but neither one turns to look at her. I smile, wincing my eyes, and lip-syncing the word sorry. She scratches her head and comes to sit next to me, wrapping her arms around my waist she looks over at the two men and then looks back at me, kissing my cheek.

"Are you going to introduce me?"

"I don't even know their names, baby."

"Why are they here?"

"They say I'm being "reimbursed" for Laurie's death."

She goes stiff and sits up leaning against me and she turns her gaze from me, while I now shrug, to them who sit absolutely still, awaiting questions.

"She died of an overdose."

They both sit silently, staring at me. I take a pull from my cigarette and hand it to her.

"They say, according to the medical report, she died of natural causes..."

I blow the smoke out and look back at them.

"...Isn't that right guys?"

"That is correct, Mr. Valentyne."

Jess puts the cigarette in the ash tray, runs her hands through my hair, and kisses me softly right next to my ear, right on end of my cheekbone, right below my temple, and she whispers.

"Are you ok baby?"

"Yeah baby, I am."

I kiss her on the lips and look back at them. They sit quietly and expressionlessly.

"So how much are we talking about here?"

"Seven hundred and fifty thousand. Once accepted we will begin your coverage and a small percentage of that will be removed and dispersed covering you and your beneficiary."

I stare blankly at Jess, and she returns the blank stare. Without speaking I ask her opinion. She smiles and nods, kissing me hard,

"You deserve it baby."

"We deserve it, jelly bean."

One removes one set of papers from his brief case and the other removes a different set of papers and a pen, they both place them on my coffee table and slide them simultaneously and slowly toward me.

I wish you never signed those.

I sign my name, and I sign her name as my beneficiary.

They're giving you medication right now, whatever you do, don't forget this.

I feel pain from somewhere outside. Sharp pain stirs me, searing inside my neck from a needle, stabbing into my tissue, burying into a vein, releasing something inside of it. I hear my heartbeat. I hear that clinking. Then I hear crackling and sizzling. I'm torn from my unconscious by more searing pain, up from my ankles, through my legs, up through my abdomen, into my chest and finally my eyes open and my jaw chomps down but this time I have something that stops me from biting down into my tongue.

The pain stops, as I'm fully conscious staring at

Sketch. My eyes are wide, and I'm completely convulsing, forcefully shaking and still completely restrained. I try to talk but I can't because of the gag over my mouth. Something is strangely placed between my teeth, larger on one end, and smaller at the other end. It has been placed in between my back molars so I can't bite down. I have cloth tied over my mouth and so I can't spit it out. It has a soft exterior and a solid interior. Something loosely rolls around on it between my teeth and gums and when I search it with my tongue, I taste blood and metal. Sketch walks around me and unties the cloth. He walks to face me and as he does, he bats me in the face with the back of his fist. I spit out the foreign object and it lands at my feet. It is a finger, with a ring on it, a diamond ring; an engagement ring. It had been severed right after the knuckle and not cleanly, it appears to be sawed off. As Sketch recovers from backhanding me, I hear that clinking, that glass clinking.

"I know. I know. Not that sanitary but I thought you'd get the point."

"Who...who...whose finger is that?"

I chatter a sentence through my jaw that uncontrollably shakes.

"What? Do you not recognize her finger, her ring? Did you suddenly forget everything again?"

"Wha..."

Sketch hits me again, following through, each knuckle tears across my cheekbone. Something just after his fist limply cuts across my nose and I hear that glassy clink.

"Let me tell you a story... There was a couple, let's call them Becky and Brandon, and they were talking to a man named Greyor when I came in the backdoor and went upstairs. When Greyor left, Becky made Brandon a stiff drink and gave him something to help him sleep because he was in so much pain. Brandon went to bed and fell into a deep sleep because he was so injured from having the shit beaten out of him. Becky went into the bathroom and started to run a bath. When she did, I went in and tied the unconscious Brandon to his bed. I went into the washroom to find Becky, naked, leaning over the tub checking the water temperature. She didn't even get the chance to see me. I forced her head in the water. When she started flailing, she brought her left hand out of the water and tried to strike me, so I stuck her hand to the wall with this..."

He pulls out a large knife; the back part of the blade has a saw on it still covered in her gore.

"...she stopped fighting for a bit, she didn't move that hand, I bet it hurt too much with these wicked teeth waiting for her to try..."

He waves the knife in my face. I hear the clinking noise.

"...I didn't wait long, after her hand was impaled, I just couldn't help myself. I skewered her quick, just filled her right up. You should've seen her shake when I first got it in her deep. She couldn't get me off, I had my hand on the back of her neck and after I got my pants off, I held her free hand behind her back, just above that beautiful ass. I just kept pushing deeper every time, watching all of her shake at every thrust...it was just overwhelming...Greyor, you should've heard that sound, oh it was beautiful. Every time I buried myself further, she would smack against the tub and this fucking necklace would just ricochet right off making this clinking sound, "ta-tink, ta-tink, ta-tink." Faster and faster, it was so fucking hypnotic, and the beauty Grey..."

He holds his wrist in front of my face and there tied on the end of silver chain to his meaty wrist is that beautiful glass heart, slightly cracked, and as it bounces, I hear that glassy clink.

"...when I let her head out of the water, she didn't scream, she couldn't...she had to catch her breath and when she did, I put her head back under. I just kept on and on and on until I was done. Not sure when she stopped moving but now that I think about... she ran out of air before I was done. No worries though Grey, I cut that finger off after she was dead and then dumped her in the tub. I turned off the water, but sadly for her, the tub wasn't full. I cleaned up, brushed my teeth, and took a piss. I went back in the bedroom and untied Brandon who was still fucking unconscious...or was he dead...did I mention the house was filling with gas from the open element on the stove and I was wearing an oxygen mask? I mean I took the mask off to brush my teeth, but after that I kept it on. I left that out, didn't I? Well fuck, which is important to the story because on my way out of the house I turned on the heat and I know; why the fuck would I turn on the heat in summer? Well, I wanted the furnace to kick over eventually and when that happened...Boom!"

He makes the motion with his hands as he finishes the sentence.

Through each bond, my thumbs fold into my fist as my fingers push straight and I free flesh from the back of my hands that now bloodily hangs on, freeing myself. I'm overtaken by impulse; his immediacy is his enemy because as quick as I tear my hands free from my bonds, they catch him. My left finds his right hand that limply hangs on to his blade disarming him; I'm now armed with it, while my right slams under his chin. He painfully folds backward biting into his tongue, stumbling. I cut my harness clean off with the knife and go to stand, but the pain from the wire and clamps in and around my ankles keeps me from going very far.

When I hit the ground, I drop the knife. I recover, pulling myself back toward the chair, trying to free my ankles. As Sketch comes in for a running kick, I slide around the chair, and he catches the metal arm with his shin. I remove the wire on my ankles and painfully unhitch the clamps that tear out some of my flesh with them. Sketch throws a punch at me, but I duck it and throw a solid hit into his ribs and then jump straight up catching his chin with my skull. As he falls, I lean down and grab the knife; spinning it in my hand so the blade is beneath my wrist and the pummel points out.

I lunge forward at him, swiping at him but he grabs a metal clipboard off a nearby table and deflects my swipe, redirecting me. Before I can recover, he swats me across the face with it. I stumble to his side and before I fall completely, he cracks the clipboard down on the back of my head. I fall hard on my stomach and when I spin to my back, he kicks the knife out of my hand and buries the clipboard into my throat. I cough violently and before I even get to move, he falls with his knees, landing brutally on my arms, so each cap crushes the inside of each of my elbows. I'm prone as he sits on my chest, slapping me over and over again with the clipboard; every hit takes a trail of crimson in the direction of the swing. I stop moving after the eighth or ninth time he takes that clipboard across my jaw. Sketch's hands glide over my bloodied face, he looks down at me, regaining his composure.

"Why couldn't you just play nice, kid?"

His hands now rest on my throat.

I smile through my bloodied mouth, and I take that smile ear to ear.

"I'm going to kill everybody you ever loved kid, you going to smile about that?"

He looks at me, awaiting a response and when I give him none he starts to squeeze.

What're you doing? Fight back.

Losing air isn't ever pleasant. Your body naturally takes it and when it is denied it fights for it, with or without your help. The blackness that reaches up at my consciousness with the more air I lose is sickening and instinctually, I struggle, but he has me completely pinned. I lose more and more of the room, as it fades; I hear the sound of heels clicking on concrete, echoing loudly. Just before I lose consciousness someone interrupts Sketch.

"Benjamin."

He releases me and the air quickly brings the light of the room back as I cough in the attempt to breathe. I look up to see a skirt and long slender legs that end with stiletto black heels that tap loudly on the cold floor. Behind her, Silk stands there looking down at me, with a slight micro expression he shows concern. As Sketch sits back, he lands on my stomach, and he loudly sighs as I roll from under him.

"What're you doing to Greyor?"

"What did it look like?"

"Benjamin, what have I told you about answering a question with a question, you know how much I hate that."

"I'm sorry Alex, but Greyor is broken, and I don't think anything we can do can get him to play along anymore. So, I'm just doing what needs to be done."

"Benjamin, I'll decide when Greyor is finished."

"Alex, don't call me Benjamin. When this goes wrong, you know who to blame."

"I'm sending Greyor to fill Mr. K's policy."

I flip over on my back just in time to see Sketch smile widely, as though satisfied with this decision.

"Alright Alex, you're the boss."

I look back at this Alex woman who seems to ignore me, talking about me like I'm not here, never once looking at me. I burn her image into my skull. Blonde hair pulled tightly into a top knot, ray ban glasses, deep green eyes, and a scar just above her top lip leading near her left nostril. I look behind her at Silk, who now is ghost white; fear painting every crevasse of his face. When he catches my gaze, he looks away apologetically.

"Increase his dosage and equip him. Give him a week and then drop him at Mr. K's house."

I feel saved by the convenience of true villainy. It would be so much easier to kill me right now but whoever Mr. K is, they seem sure I won't return, and hopefully for their sake, they're right.

The twins enter, walking past Silk, Alex, and Sketch to lift me to my feet. Sketch rises in front of me, smiling. Limply, I feign defeat as I hang in the twins grasp and suddenly I point to something behind Sketch and look to the direction I pointed. When Sketch looks where I'm pointing, I break free of the twins and hit Sketch as hard as I can in the jaw. My fist lands where jaw meets ear, and Sketch buckles to the floor, unconscious. Instantly, the twins grab at me, dragging me from the room and I don't fight. They drag me down the hall and around the corner. Hanson waits smiling with a hypodermic of something loosely hanging between his index finger and middle finger, while his thumb taps the syringes end. They bring me and hold me in front of him.

"Goodbye Greyor."

Hanson stabs the needle in my neck and within moments I find darkness and nothing else.

TWENTY FOR ONE

I wake up to the vibration of my phone. It loudly buzzes away in my pocket. I'm sitting up in the driver's seat of a car. I have no idea how I got here, how long I have been unconscious, or where I am. I drunkenly remove my phone, stumbling to hold it so I can answer the call and finally I gain enough dexterity to press answer.

"Hello Grey, you're probably wondering where you are and how long you have been out. I wouldn't try to figure it out. Also, I wouldn't try to drive away because it'll take too long to hotwire this car and even if you try you won't like what happens when it starts. You also won't have that long, by now there should be men with guns coming toward you because I told them you were coming. You have three clips and a Kevlar vest; even then, your chance of survival is slim to none. Those men who are coming work for a man named Lennox K, and he knows you're coming. He knows a lot more about you than you know about yourself. To be blunt, he doesn't like you and the only way you're getting out of this is if you kill him and all his friends – which isn't going to happen.

It would've been easier for us to just kill you but at least you can make a dent for us.

I wish I could've been there...

Love, Sketch..."

When he hangs up the windshield shatters. I grab the handle, open the door, and dive into the street as more and more gunfire tears pieces from the car. I pull my M1911A1 out and pop the clip to check if it is loaded and it is. I feed the clip back in and check my holster. I have two full clips waiting. The two men approach, unloading a MAC-10- and twelve-gauge pump action into the fender, tires, windows, doors, and body of the car. When they run out, I hear them go to reload and I rise and return fire. I fire two bullets, one and then another only a fraction of a second apart from the first, just to compensate for height. Two well-placed shots render both opponents dead. Each bullet enters into skull, dropping one, and then quickly the other. They fall at almost the same rate, smacking limply on to the concrete.

I walk toward the house they came from, vigilantly gazing around, gun up and ready. I pay no attention to my wounds because they have all but healed and are all bandaged. My hands and ankles are sore but functional as I'm already within seconds of the front door of this—somehow--familiar house in a familiar looking neighborhood. This neighborhood looks abandoned and disheveled. Most of the houses are dark with boards nailed over the windows and doors, and caution tape closing off some. This neighborhood is lost to the world and the only lights on this street are from this house. I walk into the house quietly and I hear voices, one sharply calls out when I come inside.

"Picked the wrong house to come knocking, eh guys? Poor mother fucker never had a chance."

I hear laughing and I follow it into the living room. When I walk in, five men pay no attention until one speaks up with the word,

"Fuck."

They sit at a dinner table littered with cards, half empty baggies kept company by half empty bottles and a firearm for each of them.

Like a sprinkler, I fire five shots, one after the other, following one mechanical path before returning my aim to one point. I relieve the clip, reach, and quickly feed my gun another. I'm reloaded and ready as I look from the living room up at the stairs leading to the second level. A man runs down the stairs with shotgun in hand and one shot has his lifeless corpse tumbling down the stairs toward my feet. I hear footsteps and voices following him. I step between the entrance of the living room and the staircase to the second level, and I wait. As I hear the sound of approach with the same immediacy as the last guy who fell on the stairs, I step back out and look. I fire shot after shot after shot, skipping the recoil, as three more men join the one who finally hits the bottom stair. They all crumble from head wounds, with their weapons slinking down behind them. I climb up and leap over the slowly descending corpses and make my way to the second floor.

I stop when I hit the top of the stairs and reach a new hallway with a left and a right. I hear more voices and more footsteps. I glance to the right and then take cover as the corner of the staircase explodes from a shotgun spray. I look back in the same direction, I see one man with a shotgun, and as soon as I do, I put a bullet between his eyes. I have two bullets in my clip left. I look right and quickly duck back to the staircase. Several bullets dig into the dry wall from the opposite direction. I duck and look in that direction and I feed two more into the two guys on the left. My barrel slides back. Again, only split seconds apart, because when I duck back to the staircase, I hear them drop one after the other. I eject my empty clip returning it to my holster and feed my hungry cannon a new one.

I glance right and then pull myself back to the staircase. I wait and then pop out again looking at the left side of the hallway. When it is clear I stand in the hallway, glancing left to right, I walk left, constantly looking back over to the right. I hear more voices and more footsteps, but they are coming down the stairs from above, I move to the end of the hallway, opposite the staircase to the next level, which is at the end of the right hallway. I come to a door at the end of the left hallway, and I hear voices from behind it. I kick open the door and step in and when I understand the room I fire one shot. It takes the skull off a man standing with his pants down in front of a girl. He has his back to me, but he has a MAC-10 in his hand, dropping it as he falls; she swallows and then cowers when he falls and lands in front of her, dead. I stand at the doorway but don't go out into the hall. I point my finger at her and then bring it to my lips, shushing her without words; I listen to the sound of more men bounding downstairs from the third floor.

They hit the hallway and stop, looking at their dead friends. I step out quickly and then stand back in the room.

"He's right there."

When they start moving, I step out, throwing myself into the wall across from the door as I watch the doorway explode in a hail of shotgun and machine pistol fire, sundering the doorway into shards. They don't have time to turn their fire to where I'm standing. I take three more, quick, well-placed shots, dropping three more people before standing back in the room. When I finish my seemingly endless exhale, I hear them drop. Three more dead. Three more bullets.

"Who the fuck are you?"

I look over to the half-naked girl who looks up at me puzzled and nearly paralyzed with blood splatter across her face and chest.

I smile, wink, and exit the room with my gun up and aiming, and make my way toward the staircase to take me to the third floor. I stop just before it. I quickly glance up and then gain cover. I don't see anyone, so I creep up each stair distributing my weight carefully. When I get to the top, I crouch at the last couple stairs because it is one hallway, which means I have no cover at the top of it, so I glance up at the hallway and see three doors: one door to the left, one door to the right, and one at the end of the hall. When I pull my head down past the floor of the third level, right in front of the top of staircase it comes apart in a storm of bullets, two MAC-10's spray out eating the hard wood up and out. I stand up on the third stair from the top, giving me just enough sight to see the shooters but also implicating my face and a bullet to take my head off, but like all the other targets tonight, I dispatch within seconds from each other. As soon as I see them, I shoot them. One bullet penetrates into the eye-socket of the guy in the right doorframe. Upon impact, it shatters his socket and splinters the cheekbone. He topples viciously with his head bouncing off the doorframe. Inside the same recoil, the second bullet tears into the right-side forehead of the guy in the left doorway, and as they fall, they both spray bullet after bullet, each cutting a crescent of dry wall out in different directions before they land, hard and lifeless.

One bullet left.

I know that this bullet is meant for the person waiting behind door number three. I put my phone into my hand and open my SD memory. In it I find out about Mr. K.

This policy, unlike the others, was intended to be the last one before my "retirement" or "vacation". I had failed to fill Brandon's policy now for the second time and even after what happened, and how much they increased my medication, in my opinion; they sent me after this one policy because no one had returned with it processed.

They expected the same end for me.

No one from my company had finalized this because no one could even get remotely close to him, mostly because he had his own army. Mr. K was a drug lord who had taken a policy out just in case, so that whomever he loved, or should I say whoever his beneficiary was, wouldn't be left with nothing. As I read on, I can't say I see a man like this loving much besides money. His entire operation and wealth depended on the self-destructive habits of others. He had assaulted, raped, or murdered anyone who got in his way, so I guess, if you were him, which again you are hopefully not, you too would want life insurance.

Bad choice, Lennox "The sledge" Kade, or as I would shortly come to know him, Lennox K. I would also understand why they called him "The sledge". "The sledge", is a hallway and a doorway away from me. That name and this house and this neighborhood all seem familiar; I know this place, this neighborhood, because I have been here before. I'm driven to finish this and then go back to Southstone. If they think they can just drop me off and expect me to fail, well, they haven't been paying attention, and now I'm offended. *If you want something done don't do it yourself just get someone more capable to do what the last person couldn't, isn't that right Sketch? I wonder who the last person was.* I don't know, but as I said, I woke up one day and they helped me become this guy and if they think I'm just going to lie down and let them end me, well, they're sadly mistaken.

When I'm done with Lennox, I'm coming after them. I don't run from my demons, I chase them.

That a boy.

I walk down the hallway and when I hear movement and the gauging of a shell I take cover behind the doorway to the right of the hallway, just as a twelve gauge shotgun splinters and melts the third door and wall around it. I lose count of shots. It sounds like a Benelli m4 twelve gauge, but I don't know how many shells have been fired or how many were loaded. I assume Lennox is the one firing and he is behind door number three.

I think he fired seven and maybe he has modified the shotgun to take nine but that is only if it is modified, and considering the help and situation, I assume that that shotgun is out, and he is either going to reload or is just completely without shotgun ammunition; but I can't chance it. I walk down the hallway, gun raised, ready to kick what left of the door there is, open.

I see him behind it and just before I get to raise my leg for a kick, a final shot tears from the door and catches me in the chest. I fly backward losing grip of my gun and hit the hallway floor hard, sliding backward. I gasp deeply as I'm winded and luckily my Kevlar vest has absorbed and taken the entirety of the ball barring and slug of his twelve-gauge round. My chest is burning and bruised. I don't even stand or move when Lennox opens the door and walks toward me throwing the empty shotgun aside.

"I'm going to fucking make you wish that killed you."

He charges and lifts me up easily. This man is a monster. Six three maybe six four, I have no idea what he weighs but he tosses me around like he weighs twice what I do. He throws me into one wall, and I stick into the drywall and lodge in between broken two by four. He turns and tosses me into the opposite wall. When he hits me, I realize why they call him "Sledge". His fist cuts into my flesh, separating it instantly, and the entire area around the punch swells and bleeds. It feels broken. He lifts me back up after nearly separating my head from my shoulders and charges me into the third room. We stop hard against the desk at the other end of this room. As I hit, I feel my back arch so far back over the edge of the desk as he crushes it hard against the wall, pushing the desk back, trapping the chair behind the desk firmly against the wall. He spins in place and as we turn, he throws another violent punch into me. I don't stop until I'm buried in the wall to the right of the door. He grabs my throat with his right and grabs my mangled Kevlar with his left, tearing it off. He shines off his metallic grin and then lets my throat go. He takes a quick step back and then feeds me the hardest punch I have ever received. It feels like my ribs shatter and air quickly evacuates my lungs followed by a mouth full of warm blood that I'm unable to keep in as it dribbles out over my lips. I almost cradle from that hit but somehow I manage to stay on my feet.

"Oh wait, that ain't going to remind you, is it Johnny?"

"My name is..."

He throws his hammer of a right hand straight into the bridge of my nose, and with the hit my head goes back into the wall, almost penetrating into the other room, but his hand does. It goes straight into my face, pushing it back and it doesn't stop till it punctures the wall. He pulls his hand back and grabs my hair, pulling me right into his face.

"I know who the fuck you are! I know your fucking name! Did Henry get tired of our deal?"

He steps back, pulling my face into his left hand, and after I smack off it, he steps back again and puts his right back into me, guiding me back inside the wall. My blood spills from multiple lacerations, I'm dazed and half-standing, semi-conscious, held up by the drywall and broken wall supports.

"Am I ringing any bells Johnny boy? It's too bad, we could've changed things, Henry and me. Do you have idea the value of a working girl you wouldn't have to pay? A bitch who'd let you do anything and never say shit? Well, if Henry ain't going to deal no more at least he gave me you as a parting gift."

"What're..."

He lays another fist into my chest.

You know the expression, having the shit beat out of you—that hasn't happened yet but if this continues it might—I now understand the term because something is being beaten out of me. I recognize him—from when or where I don't know—I do recognize him.

"Don't act like you don't know."

He hits me again.

"I don't know what're you're talking about."

I cough the sentence up with a mouth full of blood.

"Oh, you don't eh..."

He lifts my face back up, holding it up by my chin, I don't feign confusion, and I can't sincerely show it even when I have no idea what he is talking about.

"Here, let me help you remember Johnny boy."

He throws a fist against my face, but before I fall, he hits me again and again, pummeling me from left to right, beating me down and he doesn't stop until I'm forced through the wall into the other room. When I hit the ground with a gasp for air, I lick the back of my mouth and I feel shards of two back teeth, and as I do, I roll on my side spitting the chunks out with an entire mouthful of blood.

I hear him go back into the other room, pushing the desk out and removing something from a drawer and I hear plastic scrunching in his hand. I look in the hallway from the room I'm now in and there just within my reach, if I crawled just a bit, is my M1911A1 which I dropped when I got shot in the chest. He begins to enter the room as I drag myself toward my gun. He tosses a bag full of multi-colored pills up and down, it lands limply in his palm with every toss.

"You know, Billy is finally gonna get some fucking justice and I think...know...I know this is exactly what he had in mind."

Lennox comes from the wall with the bag of pills, wiping the dry wall dust from his shoulders and smiling a wide golden smile, until he sees me. I'm almost sitting against the wall, my gun in hand, raised and directed at his head. I exhale as he walks toward me,

"I guess you ain't going to get what's coming to you..."

He looks at me disappointingly, his big swollen hands nearly fall to his side, and he looks like he is about to lunge but is stopped, forced back, and toppling, as a bullet tears through his skull, knocking the back out of it. The gore and crimson cascade across the gaping hole and remaining wall behind him. My M1911A1 barrel slide rackets back letting me know I'm empty. I let my hand fall to the side as the gun spins smoking on my finger, and with my left I pull myself to sitting. I spit a stream of blood against the door frame, and I take a very long, deep breath that seems to go on and almost take the light from the back of my eyes. I avoid my unconsciousness as I shake, my mouth dribbles more blood. I take a moment, maybe several moments before I move again. I allow the pain to cut across me and the adrenaline to leave before I try and stand but when I do, I'm greeted by more pain which only helps because at least I don't lose consciousness in this daze.

I close the slide of my gun and holster it. I slowly rise. Pushing from the floor, using the doorframe to support me, I slide upwards with my spine against it. When I get to standing, I don't move, I spit more blood, and then look around the corner. I use the walls to keep me standing. I'm swaying and disoriented but moving forward. I have to get out of this house. When I get to the staircase down, I take several more moments before I try to descend. Finally, I take the first mangled stair down and then another followed by another. I'm not as vigilant because when I reach the second floor, I walk right in the path of the girl from earlier but this time she is armed with a shotgun, aiming it at me.

"Stop!"

She barks at me. She is now dressed and shaking. Shotgun raised and incorrectly aimed because if she does take a shot the kick back will hurt her. I do what she requests momentarily as I deeply exhale, looking up at her beyond the facial swelling. I blink several times and then spit blood before trying to speak,

"If you're going to shoot, shoot. If not, get the fuck out of my way."

She gauges the shotgun,

"I will."

"I don't doubt it. But either do it or I'll make you swallow that barrel if you don't get the fuck out of my way."

I spit more blood and wobble forward it.

She stands her ground, holding the shotgun, not lowering it, still appearing that any moment she is going to fire.

When I'm within arm's reach, she lowers the shotgun and steps out of my way, dropping it.

"Please don't..."

"I'm not going to hurt you."

I walk by her and when I get to the top of the staircase to the first level I stumble and trip, barreling down the staircase and when I get to the bottom I sit up.

"Fuck."

She comes down behind me.

"You can't even walk, here, let me help you."

I turn and look up at her.

"Are you crazy? I shot your boyfriend in the head— I killed everyone in the house, except you— and you're going to help me stand?"

"Honey, he ain't my boyfriend, and I'm just glad you didn't kill me. The quicker I get you out of here, the quicker I can, understand? Now, take my hand?"

I give her my arm and she tugs me to my feet.

"Who are you anyways?"

"Just a guy."

She looks at me puzzled as she helps me to the front door.

"A guy who walks in and kills twenty-one people? You're not just a guy."

"It is a long story, and we don't have time."

My face swells and my body numbs. When you get hit this much you become use to the sting.

Maybe not hit by a man like Lennox, but it makes it easier to shrug it off, or at least stay conscious.

She looks back into the living room and then into the kitchen.

"Do you mind if I stay, like, I don't want to go with you, but if you're going to leave everything the way it is, mind if I take it?"

"Be my guest but hurry up."

She smiles, looking back eagerly.

I look in the kitchen and see a large red metal kettle, sitting on the top of a dirty stove. She goes to leave, making her way into the living room but I grab her arm and tug her back.

"This house have a backyard?"

"Yeah."

"Does it have a shed?"

"Yeah?"

"Ok be quick, get what you want and be back here in two minutes."

She looks at me, trying to figure out what I'm up to, and then she smiles and takes off.

I limp towards the kitchen and past the corpses and past the stove over the dirty linoleum floor. I walk to the back door, which is on the other side of the kitchen.

I open one door and then a screen door and stumble out into the night, this backyard has no light, and now as I stumble off a broken concrete stair I land hard on my hands, catching myself before pushing from the ground. From the light of the kitchen, I make out the sheet metal shed, and I open the loud creaking, awkwardly opening, double doors. I search around a lawn mower and gardening tools and find what I'm looking for; a jerry can of gasoline. I walk back toward the house and know I have to leave very soon.

I don't know who is coming, but someone is, and I can't be here when they get here. I get back inside and close the doors with my sleeves. I grab the kettle of the stove and fill it with gasoline; I get most of the jerry can in it just before it spills out. I slide the jerry can off to the side and put the lid of the old metal kettle on. I put the kettle down and look under the sink and in the cupboards. I look for any aerosol cans; anything with an explosive label warning. I find two cans of air freshener that clearly state if heated they will explode. I put them on the stove. I turn on the gas element and light the gas with my Zippo. I place the kettle on the burner and walk out of the kitchen. I walk into the main hallway and there, in front of the door; the girl waits with a large duffle bag on her shoulder. She smiles at me and extends her hand.

"What's in there?"

"Everything of worth in this house."

"Fits in one bag, that's convenient, let's go."

"What were you doing?"

"Let's just go."

I go to walk out the door, but she stays next to me, helping me.

"I'll get you to your ride."

We open the front door and walk out into the night. I stumble off the porch and almost fall but her weight keeps me standing. As we walk toward my car, I realize that I can't take it, and then I realize there are more cars than when I went in. A split second from that realization I lose my balance because the girl helping me hits the ground gyrating as harpoons and wire find home in her chest. While she convulses on the ground, I stand up on my own, smiling. Three retrievers walk toward us, one draws a gun, an .45 USP tactical and the other two walk toward me with tasers raised. I take a step back. The one retriever walks toward the unconscious girl, the one that holds the gun, and he aims at her. He doesn't realize he is between me and the other two retrievers. I kick his arms to the right; a shot goes off; it digs in the ground near her arm. I lunge towards him and then step to his left and pull him back to the right as the other two aim at me and fire, but the harpoons strike their gun-wielding friend.

He hits the ground, and I don't wait for them to eject cartridges, I move toward them and as I do, they don't try to eject, they just come at me. As the first one gets close to me, I catch him mid run, and I kick hard into his right inner leg, right at the knee, and step back. He trips and stumbles and falls in front of me. His friend trips over him, his head falling toward me, up and over his downed friend. In one fluid motion I catch his head and violently snap his neck. He falls like a weight on his friend and pins him. I kick down hard on the back of that guy's neck, he goes limp from the first stomp, and I turn quick to someone behind me. The last retriever, the one with the gun and he has it pointed at my face.

"I should have done this a long time ago."

I look him in the eyes and I watch as I see his eyes squint and the skin pulls tight around them, like when you smile.

I close my eyes.

I hear two shots go off, but I don't feel anything and when I open my eyes, he has his back to me and there is a knife lodged in it. I see the girl drop and as he spins toward me, I pull the knife out and sidestep him. With my left hand I catch his wrists and swipe across his throat with the knife severing the artery so that blood geysers from the large slit in his nylon mask. He releases the gun and falls hard clutching at his throat. I watch him bleed, unflinching, I just watch as he dies. Suddenly, I'm woken by a large bang, and I see light burn from inside the house as fire washes into the first floor.

I go to the girl who is already dead, and I kneel down and close her eyes whispering in her ear,

"Thank you."

I grab the duffle bag and open it. In it, several sacks of cocaine, pills which I can only assume to be MDMA or ecstasy, a couple of bags of marijuana, several wads of cash and a bottle of whisky. I take the whisky and cash. I close the bag and drop it next to one of the retrievers. I take the two extra clips from the one with the .45 USP tactical and I take the cartridge from the gun, but leave the gun with him, and I walk toward the car I woke up in. I look around for signs of life and no one is nearby, and no one is coming. No cops have been called. No witnesses. The neighborhood is dead like everyone in it. I look under the car, for explosives, for something rigged to the starter...nothing. I open the door and pop the hood and look around the ignition and around the engine...nothing.

Sketch lied. I close the hood and walk to the driver's side door putting the cash and whisky down on the passenger seat. I sit down in the driver's seat and take out the three USP cartridges. The one from his gun has seven bullets left; I refill one of my empty clips. I throw his empty cartridge in the back seat. I empty the other two out and reload my two empty clips, leaving six free bullets without a cartridge to call home. I put the bullets in my pocket and throw the other two cartridges into the back seat. I put my gun and full cartridges back in my holster.

I grab the whisky and open it. I take a large swig and let it burn its way down my throat. I take another one, gargle with it, and then spit it out on the ground outside. Blood and whisky splash on the pavement. When I go back to sitting, I look in the rear-view mirror and realize the retrievers have the same company Ford Crown Victoria as the one I woke up in. I grab the cash and the whisky.

I walk back to the corpses and search each retriever. The one on top of the other...no keys, the one underneath him...bingo. I walk back to their car and open the door. I throw the cash and whisky on the seat and throw the keys in the ignition. I start the car and look back to the house which is now completely ablaze. I throw the car into drive and slowly drive away. I don't look back once on the massacre I've left behind. My chest and face are sore but I'm very much alive and surprisingly very conscious now. I turn street after street, looking at the abandoned houses, and every single one is familiar, but I have no memory, just déjà vu. I need to figure out where I am. When I do, I'm going back to Southstone.

When I get to my next turn my stomach sinks and my chest hurts. The pain in my chest gets worse as I lay eyes on a house. I recognize it, this one more than the others because I'm compelled to stop. I'm six blocks from Lennox's house and people still live on this street. I pull up not even an inch from the curb and park.

I sit up, staring at the door. I see someone in the living room window as they open the curtains and look out and then disappear. A moment later the porch light flicks on and the front door opens, and a woman walks out on the porch and stares at me. A moment later a man comes out and puts his arm around her. I recognize them. I've seen them before. Years ago, but I recognize them even though I only saw them for a moment. It is the couple from the motel room the night I killed Christopher. Even though I've only seen this couple once, I've seen that girl before. That girl is from my memories. She walks off the step and walks toward the car. I don't wait. I throw the car into drive and squeal off, leaving her in the rear view.

In this moment, I know I do have a life or whatever is left of it, waiting for me somewhere here, whether any of this makes sense or not. Whatever got me in this situation started in this neighbourhood and I'm going to find out who I am. The best place to start looking is where it all started, somewhere here, this is how I'll start my "vacation", not "retirement", and I'll be back at Southstone in no time.

I take my phone out and call the only friend I know I have. The phone rings a couple times and then he answers,

"Grey? You're alive! I don't understand, didn't you go after Lennox, how're..."

"Lennox is dead. Silk, where are you?"

HOMECOMING

the sun beats down on my face, cooking over the cracking scabs. I'm baking in the afternoon sun, stretched out on the hood of the Crown Victoria I took from the retrievers; waiting in the almost empty parking lot of a clothing store named Cheyenne. Silk asked me to meet him here,

"Grey."

I open my eyes and sit up and I see Silk walking toward me. His hands outstretched in what looks like his eagerness to hug me. His smile is almost blinding as I squint from under my hand shielding out the bright sunlight.

"You look like shit. How do you feel?"

"Off."

"Sorry I made you wait – I'm here on a job; work has been keeping me busy. Plus, we wouldn't want the company catching up with us yet."

"How long has it been since we talked on the phone?"

"About ninety-six hours…"

"Fuck. Really?"

"Yeah. Why?"

I feel groggy and somewhat confused. The swelling in my face has gone down but the pain is still very present, and each wound is tender.

I reach into my pocket and pull out the Zippo; the medication bottle rolls on the back of my hand, and I feel the pills inside shift.

Silk smiles and reaches for his cigarettes; he pulls two from the pack, throwing one to me and one to his lips. He sits down beside me and nudges me with his shoulder.

I roll it around in my hand, the light bounces off the stainless steel shell, refracting light into my eyes. With a snap of my fingers the lid opens, and with a snap of my thumb I bring flame to a blackened wire wick.

"You haven't taken your medication, have you?"

"Nope."

I pull the flame to my cigarette, the paper peels back with fresh ember. I put the flame to Silks cigarette and watch the same process. I take a deep breath and blow the smoke slowly out, watching it disperse in the breeze, shapelessly.

"You're lucky to be alive Grey."

Oddly, when he says that, it seems foreign; the name sounds wrong.

"What is my real name?"

"Greyor?"

"Silk, you and I both know that isn't my real name."

"You have to stop this Grey, things have changed."

I smile, blowing smoke from between my teeth.

"You don't have to tell me that."

"Grey, they don't want you dead anymore. They want you back. Lennox...you weren't supposed to live through that, but you did, which proves something. You didn't have to, you could have taken off, but you did what they sent you to do..."

"So, they love me again...how nice...I'll send them flowers. Bottom line is I'm starting to remember. They told me what would happen if I did that."

"It is different now Grey, I can prove it, you can come back."

"And if I don't want to?"

"Then they will kill you."

"They will try..."

"Grey, you've been lucky..."

I look at him wide eyed and offended.

"...and maybe yeah...a bit more than lucky...you have a talent...but you can't kill all of them."

"You want to bet on that?"

"You'll be betting with my life Grey...I can't help you. You need to let it go. They needed proof and they got it. Now we can go back to the way it was."

I shake my head, chuckling.

"Way it was? Which way is that exactly?"

"Our work, the only thing we're good at."

"The only thing we know."

"The only thing I have ever known."

"But what about me Silk? You know damn well that

this isn't all I have ever known. It is only what I can remember."

"So, what, you can't remember who you were, it isn't who you are now."

"I beg to differ. Whoever I was is coming back and nothing can stop it. Not even me."

"Grey. You have to let it go. You have nothing left. Trust me, it is all gone."

"How do you know that?"

I slide off the hood and stand in front of him.

"I know. Grey, I'm sorry. It...it... is gone."

He slides off standing in front me.

"It doesn't feel like it."

"Do you remember anything?"

"When I do remember it's only flashes of a life at most, at times entire memories but nothing connecting them. Maybe, scenes, and nothing tangible, mostly scattered memories. I remember a name and places and faces. Not who and what they are or what they mean to me or anything about them except for names."

"Greyor, I know it is hard, but you have nowhere else to go. You need the company as much as they now need you."

"Riley remembered."

"Who's Riley?"

"Hanson's pet."

"Oh. Her. So, what if she remembered?"

"I might."

"It'll just make things harder."

"Silk. You know a lot more about me than I know about myself. What does it matter to you, if I remember it?"

"Because, you'll hurt me, probably even kill me if you remembered. Grey, I don't want to help you remember."

"Whatever you did, I don't care. I'm what you're keeping me from. Silk, I can't go back, I can't work for them. I can't keep doing what I've doing. Help me."

"Grey. Please just let it go. You can keep working for Grim. You killed Lennox, for fuck sakes you killed everyone protecting him...the company won't kill you...not after that...you have no idea what he was worth and how his death proved how much they can benefit from you. So, what, some girl remembers a life she had before Grim associations, and look how that turned out for her?"

"She is dead."

"Yep."

"Yeah, because Sketch shot her with a shotgun from point blank and she bled out in my arms."

"And they could do the same to you. Greyor, just because you haven't died yet, don't think you can't. If you try and leave, they won't stop coming after you until your dead, but if you go back to them you will live. I can send you to Alex, she'll make sure of it. I'll make sure of it."

"You keep calling me Greyor. I know my name isn't Greyor."

"It's just a name."

"No, because a name has a life attached to it, and Greyor has Grim associations and nothing else. While Johnny, on the other hand, has a life and things attached to it."

"You're not Johnny."

"I'm Greyor when I'm on the medication. What happens when I don't take the medication?"

"You're not yourself."

"Because Greyor isn't who I am."

"It is. You're not Johnny. Johnny is dead."

"When I take the pills, he is dead."

"Greyor, you're not Johnny."

"How do you know? Do you know who I am?"

You're Johnny.

"Who do you think you are?"

"Johnny Valentyne."

"Johnny Valentyne is dead. Are you a dead man? Greyor, I was wrong, I know what I said about the medication but at least you can focus when you're on it. Look at yourself, you're a mess."

My only friend has turned on me.

"Silk. You need to tell me who I am."

"Greyor, you don't want to know. Let it go."

Both our smokes are done, and we stand there flicking them opposite directions.

"I want to know. Tell me."

"What you had has moved on. The life you had ended a long time ago. If you try and go back, you will find nothing."

"Silk. Stop with the generalities. You said the Zippo was mine. I used to smoke and have picked it back up."

"Partly my fault."

He smiles his pretty smile, holding back the truth from behind that shiny grin.

"I remember this place, it is familiar, so was Lennox's neighbourhood, I'm from around here."

"Yes. This is where you grew up."

"And?"

"And what?"

"What else?"

"This is where the company recruited you."

"Did I go willingly?"

"No."

"Then they didn't recruit me, did they?"

"Does that change the fact that you work for them?"

"No, it doesn't change the fact that they force me

to work for them."

"You had a life which you abandoned."

Lies

"I didn't abandon anything. I was forced to."

"Why does it matter? You are who you are now. Who you were is long gone and the people you didn't abandon forgot about you."

"Prove it."

"I can't."

"Yes, you can."

"How do you know?"

"Because if you are so certain that I have nothing then you could prove it."

"Would it matter? Even if I could prove you have nothing? Would that stop you?"

"Probably not."

"Then we are stuck. I want you to come back. You don't want to come back. I have to do what I'm here to do. You can do what you want."

"What are you here to do?"

"Fill a policy. My job. What you used to do."

"A woman?"

"Of course."

"How is she supposed to die?"

"Drug overdose as usual."

"Her beneficiary?"

"Her boyfriend."

"Her name?"

"Does it matter?"

He looks away, fiddling in his pocket for his cigarettes.

"Does it matter if I know?"

Silk doesn't answer, he just pulls his pack out and offers me a cigarette and after I accept, he grabs one for himself nodding for me to light it. As I light it, he draws a big breath in and then speaks,

"Of course not."

"Well, what is her name?"

He takes another breath in and smiles and then blows smoke out.

"Jessica Mackenzie."

When he finishes her name my heart sinks and something inside me explodes, I'm overwhelmed by something foreign, by something resurfacing and quickly. I step back. He doesn't look at me. I swallow hard as this new feeling pains me beyond distraction. I know that name. It means something to me. I can't remember who she is but the mention of her name and what he intends to do, have me completely overwhelmed by anger and defence.

Whoever she is I don't want her to die.

"I know that name."

"Greyor, you don't know her."

"Johnny does."

"Greyor, you have to let it go. Come back to Grim. I'll call Alex. We will help you…"

"You can't help me. I want to remember, and you and Grim both obviously don't want that."

"I'm sorry for what happened but it's too late for that guy, it doesn't have to be too late for you."

"It's already too late for me Silk, you know that…and I know that."

He lets out a sigh, finishing his smoke and he draws another one a second after he throws away that one.

"Don't say I didn't try."

"I won't."

I light the cigarette he gave me earlier and I light his.

"It could be worse, right?"

I look at him pulling in the smoke.

"I could be dead."

I blow the smoke out and then look up to see his new expression. He has dropped his cigarette and has a knife in his hand, blowing smoke out in a furious exhale, lunging at me. I catch his hand that holds the knife and stop his motion. I spit my cigarette out and hold him there,

"I thought you didn't remember; I didn't want to have to do this."

"Do what, what're you doing?"

He pushes the knife closer to my chest by adding

his other hand to the hilt, but I hold him off, and only barely.

He is trying to kill me, trying to bury that blade into my chest.

"I'm sorry I killed her, I didn't know you, and it is my job. I'm sorry...for what Grim did to you, it's a rough deal, I would take back what I did if I could, but I can't."

"Silk, drop the knife, I don't want to do this..."

"No, but you have to. If you don't, I'll kill her too. This is what I know...it is all I know...this is who I am. I don't have a life to go back to...even if you do."

He forces the knife closer and closer, and every bit of my strength goes to restraining his motion and the direction of the knife. Even with all of my strength, the knife gets closer to my stomach. His eyes water and his expression is regretful, but he continues to force the blade, and I have run out of sympathy or empathy. I don't care what he means to me; what he's done for me; I'm not letting him stab me. With my fists on his hands and both his hands on the knife I take a quick step back and reposition my hands and change the direction of the blade. Even with his hands on the knife the blade points at him, and I don't let him drop the knife. I force his hands back and take a step forward. Tears stream down his face and his teeth grind. He exhales as the blade punctures his skin. He chokes as the blade disappears half way into his gut. He loses strength as the blade is now fully submerged up to the handle in his stomach. I catch him as he falls and hold him standing. As his blood spills on to my shirt, I watch the life leave his face. First his skin changes pigment and then his eye color fades. Not noticeably, like extreme pigment changes, but rather subtle and faded. He whispers,

"Nothing is cement or solid, everything is fluid and transitory. The moment we forget that, is the moment we hold on too long. You say you're Johnny Valentyne..."

"I was."

"...Wasn't he really good with a knife?"

"I don't know."

"... If you are him, tell me, where did you learn to use a gun?"

"The company taught me."

"... and they taught you to be a marksman?"

"Yes."

"...Are you sure about that?"

I don't remember being trained.

"No."

"Please don't leave me in this fucking parking lot."

I drag him to the passenger side of the car and open the door. I push him into the seat and reposition him, fixing his posture, making it look like he is sleeping, sitting up but sleeping. I take off my jacket and holster and put them on the roof of the car. I take of my shirt off and wipe my hands of his blood. There is so much blood; with every wipe it seems to just smear over and over in the same place. It takes me about minute and my shirt soaked to get all the blood from my hands. I put my bloodied shirt over Silk's wound. I reattach my holster to my bare chest and then throw my jacket back on. I close the door and lock the car electronically. I walk toward Cheyenne and enter. When I get in it is quiet with background music so subtle that I can't make out the song. It smells nice and the temperature is perfect, a perfect balance of hot and cold. The balance of too hot outside but not air-conditioned freezing in here. I look to my hands that I've cleaned most of the blood from. The only place it still exists is on the back of my finger nails where nail meets skin, staining into the crevasses.

"Can I help you?"

From my hypnosis I'm snapped out by a voice, a painfully familiar sweet voice, one I have heard many times, and it calms my stampeding heart beat. I look up from my hands to a robustly slender female with one hand on her hip and in a mannequin like stance. Her hair falls in front of her left eye, but before it covers her vision, she tosses it back with a flick of her head. When she returns, she is smiling. Her lips pucker momentarily in their fullness before returning her white grin. When she looks at my face, hers moderately winces, trying to understand if who she sees is who she thinks she sees. She shakes her head as her jaw drops momentarily before closing her mouth and shifting in her stance. I walk a step forward and she shakes the idea of recognition.

"This is going to sound really lame, but don't I know you?"

"I don't think so."

I shine a clever smile, as though I'm fibbing innocently.

She shakes her head and laughs.

"Sorry...what do you need?"

"Under shirt and a dress shirt."

She stares at my chest that is exposed through my open jacket. Her eyes don't move off my waistline where my belt buckle digs into my abdomen. My pants hang showing the contours of waist and lower abdominal muscles. I look up from what she is looking at and try to catch her gaze. She bites her lip and looks back up at me, then realizes what she's doing, and smiles a wide pretty smile.

"This way."

She spins and quickly walks into aisles of clothes, nearly knocking over a display. She laughs and continues. I follow her, watching her hips sway as each leg strongly connects with the ground, springing to the next step. She looks back and smiles at me, I grin cutely, raising my eyebrows, slightly shaking my head. Low cut jeans and a low cut tank top have me distracted and enthralled. I don't take my eyes off her; her frame, her ass, the small of her back, even her swaying shoulders as she strides down the aisle. With every step I hear the smack of her flip flop on her bare foot. She grabs an undershirt off a shelf and then a white wrinkle free dress shirt off a hanger.

"You can try them on back here."

She stops at a set of royal blue curtains that cover a room attached to this one. She hands me the clothes and I smile, walking past the curtain. When I enter the room, a full sized mirror waits to greet me but I don't look at it, I can see my feet and my eyes slowly transcend up its surface and I can see myself peripherally. But before I have the chance to look at myself, I feel hands around my waist, they slowly ascend to my chest, and I feel her hug me from behind. Her breasts push up against my back and she holds me tightly. I look back to greet her eyes and smile. Her unimaginably gorgeous hazel retinas strikingly overwhelm me as they gloss over moistly. I turn in her hug as she slowly pushes my coat off and it quietly hits the floor.

"Tell me something, if I don't know you, how come

you have the exact same tattoos as my dead boyfriend?"

Her hands glide over my chest and rest on my belt buckle pulling me into her.

"I don't know."

She looks from my face to my gun and holster.

"What is that for?"

"Protection."

"From what?"

"My work is dangerous."

"I can tell by your face. What do you do?"

I drop the shirts as she pushes me backward and continues until we stop against the mirror, I hear my bare back stick and crack it as she stops me hard against it.

"I'm in insurance."

"What's your name?"

"Johnny."

Her face cringes as tears well but stand still.

"Tell me something Johnny, you have his name, you look like him, you talk like him, you feel like him and you have his tattoos. How do I not know you? I mean, sure, he had more scars on his face, but you have the same ink in the same place. The weird thing, I buried my Johnny over six years ago."

"That settles it, I can't be your Johnny, do I look like a dead man?"

"Yes."

She pushes up against me hard. I see frustration and anger wash over her face as the tears still don't fall and then she lifts her face to mine, right next to my face, her lips and nose touch mine and then she speaks.

"Only one way to know if you're him."

I innocently and unconsciously smile,

"And what way is that?"

She grabs my hair and pulls my face into hers. Her lips push hard against mine and we kiss slowly. Every slight retracting of lips brings them in more as our tongues glide from each other's mouths. I pull her into me as she places her hands on mine and forces them on to her ass, she then undoes my belt buckle and before it is completely open, she pushes herself from me.

"You're not wearing a shirt; I don't want to make you uncomfortable, it is only fair."

I pull her tank top over her and her beautiful breasts bounce out, barely held back by a jade coloured florally deckled bra. She smiles as she kisses me. I pull back and smile.

"Fair is fair."

I snap my fingers at her bra strap with my thumb and index finger on the different pieces that hold it on. It snaps off in behind and loosely her breasts fall out. I pull it off and continue kissing her. She pushes me hard against the mirror and kisses my neck, slowly descending to my chest, and then down over every abdominal muscle before bypassing my belly button to my gut. She goes to her knees and completely disconnects my belt, pulling down my pants and underwear down in one motion. My head hits hard against the glass as she takes me in her mouth. Her hands glide up my legs and grab each of my ass cheeks, ramming my crotch into her face before pulling back and returning. My eyes roll back into my head and this is the first time I have felt pleasure in what feels like an eternity. Every pain, every problem seems to disappear. Time disappears as she continues.

When it is too overwhelming, I stop her, pulling her to stand. I grab at her jeans and unbutton the top, tearing them off, greeted instantly by a matching jade coloured floral thong. I help her out of her jeans and glide my hands up the back of her legs as she presses down on my head. Running her fingers into my hair I drop her thong to her knees and lift her by each hip, throwing each leg, on each of my shoulders and begin to stand. I throw my head under her stretching thong so that its elastic is on the back of my skull as I lift her up on the wall and drive my mouth into her. Licking ravenously, consuming all of her in my mouth. She balances herself by forcing her hands on the back of my neck and shoulders. She gasps and digs her nails into my shoulders tearing forth flesh. Small ink lets of crimson dribble down my back. She is now sitting against the wall with her legs over my shoulders and I'm standing, eating vigorously, like I'm starving.

"Oh God, baby, I've missed you."

She pants. Every breath in becomes shorter and shorter. Every return of my tongue paralyzes her as she desperately tries to balance herself through the pleasure. She moans my name, and God's, and to be honest I don't know who gets mentioned more. This goes on till she uncontrollably gyrates and pulls me hard against her, burying my mouth and suffocating me in her. She calls my name loudly and goes limp. All of my strength goes into holding her up as I kiss her there softly. I lift her up, bringing my head from out and under its lace prison and I help her stand. I remove her thong completely, and lift her up again, but this time I bring her waist to mine and I enter savagely, forcing her hard into the wall next to the mirror.

Her nails dig into my back again and she bits down hard on my lip as I thrust into her. Over and over, I thrust, continuing the same repetition over and over again until her nails dig further, unearthing flesh from bleeding scratches on my back and she releases my lips to inhale uncontrollably.

I continue through her uncontrollable panting and

gyration until she does it again and again, resuming the same process over and over again. She shudders on top of me, losing grip of me constantly, and with every thrust I bring her back and force her harder into the wall until she loses strength again and again. She can barely hold on to me, but I keep her up and continue entering her furiously. She pushes from my face and smiles as sweat drops down her brow rolling from under her hair that now sticks to her face. She kisses me and then pulls away, smiling again.

"Come for me baby."

Instinctually, I pull out and she pushes from me dropping to her knees taking me back in her mouth, she glides her hands down my chest, over my stomach before pulling me in. I momentarily go weak as I release into her mouth, and she swallows every drop. I fall backward, smashing into the already cracked mirror. She pulls herself to me, kissing her way back to my mouth. Up from my belly, over my abdominals and over my chest, up over my neck back to my lips where she pulls away, panting and smiling.

"I've missed you so much."

"I've missed you…"

I hear the sound of a chime, and she looks at me wide eyed before smiling. We both grab for our clothes, desperately trying to dress because someone else has entered the store. She is dressed and walking out from the curtains and calls out making her presence known to whoever wandered in to the store. I pull on my pants and do my belt back. I remove my holster and pull the under shirt over. I then pull on my brand new white wrinkle free dress shirt and button it closed. I put my holster back on and then my dress jacket. As I finish dressing, trying to look at myself in the shattered mirror I hear her talking,

"Steven, what're you doing here?"

"I came to surprise you, take you to lunch."

"Oh ok, well, I have a customer trying some clothes on, but I'll close up after."

"You, ok? You look really warm, you're sweating."

"Yeah, I'm amazing; give me a second ok babe?"

I hear her flip flop back toward the dressing room. She comes in under the curtains and stands in front of me fixing her hair.

"That shirt looks really good on you."

"Thank you."

"Are you staying in town?"

"Who is that guy?"

She goes wide eye and then cringes.

"That's my boyfriend Steven...wow, long story, this doesn't change anything...I mean...I didn't know you were..."

"I have to go. I'm ready to pay."

She looks at me disappointingly, waiting and

wanting some explanation, waiting for anything except my silence. I walk by her with the intention of leaving and she stops me.

"I don't know what is going on...whatever happened to you...I don't care...you're home now and we will work it out, ok? You're him, tell me please...Johnny?"

"Yeah, I think...I don't know...I can't remember...I'm sorry...I have to go."

She cringes, holding back the tears trying to pull me back but she can't hold me. I walk out and I'm greeted by Steven. I push past him, excusing myself, smiling widely. He gives me a dirty look as I wait at the cash. She comes out of the change room pushing past him, hiding the tears,

"Jess, are you ok?"

She nods making her way behind the cash. She pushes a bunch of numbers on the register and speaks up through a choked sentence.

"One white dress shirt, one white under shirt...One hundred and ten dollars...please."

She looks up at me, smiling, her eyebrows relax when she sees my smile.

"Is that it?"

I grab the wad of cash, Lennox's cash, and take out two hundred dollars. I pass her the money.

"Keep the change."

I look at Steven who looks lost and angry. I look back to Jess and her smile, as she doesn't take her eyes off me.

"Goodbye Jess."

I turn and walk out.

"Johnny!"

"Yeah?"

As I turn, she looks at me, her eyes glazed and watery and then she looks at Steven before looking back at me.

"Do you want a receipt?"

She chokes as the last part of that sentence comes out.

"No, I'm good, but thanks. Hey, Steven...its Steven, right?"

Steven perks up, taking his attention off Jess and staring at me,

"Yeah, what?"

"Take care of her."

I turn and begin to walk out as Steven turns and questions Jess,

"Who the fuck is that?"

Jess doesn't look at Steven, I can feel her eyes on my back,

"That's Johnny."

Steven looks at me, and then back to Jess and I hear the last part of the conversation as the door closes behind me,

"The Johnny? But I don't understand, he is…"

The door shuts and I don't hear what Steven says.

I walk toward my company car. Inside it, Silk is sitting up, staring out over the parking lot. He looks like he is sleeping but he isn't. I strut toward my car in my brand new white shirt tugging at it, playing with it; I'm even proud of it. I go to the driver's side door and hop in. I turn the ignition and put the car into drive. I hear something that resembles the rumbling of thunder before heavy rain, I look up, and the sky is clear. I look straight out over the parking lot and toward me a gorgeous machine slowly rolls. Some sort of muscle car. Its engine rumbles loudly, purring with power, awaiting more acceleration. The car turns slightly and rolls in front of me.

I catch the drivers face. A man in his mid to late twenties with expensive sunglasses on slowly rolls by and he smiles at me. When he sees me acknowledging him, he peels out, crushing the accelerator, leaving a trail of foul smelling rubber in his wake. I follow him. He drives frantically through intersection after intersection until we arrive on to the highway. When he gets on the highway, I have trouble keeping up. My car cannot compete with the sheer power of his, but fortunately for me, he goes to exit at a rest stop slowing down, and I follow him. He pulls into a place called "Charlies", a rest stop diner. He parks and gets out and walks in as I drive up.

I park and sit up in the driver seat, staring at this rest stop. I turn the car off and look over at the lifeless Silk who stares off at nothing. I apologize and remove the cigarettes from his jacket. I reposition him and then I take a deep inhale.

I'm detached and confused. Unsure of the road I have chosen to take. I don't remember enough to go back to. What I know is that I'm more than what the company wants me to be. I may be without memories, but something forced me here, something deep down, something that has been clawing its way out since I woke up in a hospital bed, and medication or not, it has been impossible to ignore. I could drive away and run but I would never know. With or without the medication I can't ignore who I am, that guy, waiting on the inside that won't let go, and every second away from the medication I get closer to being him. Greyor may be who I became, but Greyor isn't who I am. I turn off the car and get out. I lock the door electronically and walk toward the diner, toward my answers. Whoever brought me here works for Grim, no coincidence. Whoever he is, he wants to talk, or do something else, but as the time passes my concentration begins to leave me.

I have to take a piss. I'm going into that diner

whether it's a good idea or not.

I walk into the diner. When I enter people eating their lunch look up and notice me and the only one who doesn't give me any attention is my friend who sits at the bar kitchen staring at a menu.

Everything is hazy and I feel more detached than ever, it is a problem just to concentrate on where I am and what I'm doing here, but I press on. Walking by every booth and every stool, my focus is broken by a loud, friendly voice,

"Can I help you son?"

"Washroom?"

"Keep going that way, first door on your right."

A large man in a dirty white apron smiles behind big bottle cap glasses. I nod, smile and continue as the need to urinate becomes impossible to ignore. When I get into the washroom, I'm instantaneously distracted by the mirrors above several sinks. As I walk to the first mirror the dizziness gets worse. I stumble and catch myself on the corners of the sink pulling myself up and bringing my face up.

I stand there staring at my reflection. I look into my brown eyes but as my eyes focus, I don't recognize anything. I don't recognize myself. My face doesn't remind me of anything, except one singular feeling, falsification. Everything about my face is wrong, I don't know it or recognize it. I don't remember who I am or who I was. I don't remember the last time I looked at myself and I don't remember what I looked like, but in this shirt, I look good.

Everyone has an idea of what they look like, and I guess I have never imagined what I looked like but whoever I'm looking at isn't who I thought I was. His calm eyes considerately and compassionately stare past me. I'm detached and more disoriented then when I walked in. My heart pounds and my head aches with every second I spend staring at this stranger. I try to remember and try and focus but the more I do, the more nauseous I get, the more I can't remember, and then something bounds past that; I really have to piss.

I turn from the mirror and run into the stall directly across from that mirror. I kick up the toilet seat with my foot and pull my dick out and begin to empty out my bladder as the stall door closes behind me. I urinate and continue to for what feels like an eternity, and my mind clears. I sway to make swirling motions into the bowl water. In my moment of relief, I barely pay attention to the footsteps that loudly echo in the washroom. I'm almost out of urine when I look up to see a crimson splatter on the wall in front of me and in its center, is a hole where a slug dug in, I don't even hear the gun go off. I grab my gun just as a bullet tears across my other arm. I drop and spin, firing. Each bullet I squeeze out punches through the stall like paper and shatters a mirror and within a second every sink is full of glass. Now I'm lying on the floor between the toilet and stall door with my gun raised and smoking. I fired six shots before hitting the ground. My dick fell back in my pants, and I deeply finish my exhale and when I go to inhale, I unintentionally speak, not much more than a whisper but I speak,

"What the fuck?"

When I go to breathe in, my nostrils burn as I'm overwhelmed by a sick stench of piss, shit, and mildew as my gun hand firmly holds my M1911A1 in the direction of my shooter. I'm hyperventilating and the shock is just as horrible as the stench I can smell. Something pollutes the air, and I don't remember where I am or how I got here.

The only thing on my mind is a smell, just a stench...